President
★ of the ★
Whole
Sixth
Grade

Copyright © 2015 by Sherri Winston
Excerpt from *The Sweetest Sound* copyright © 2016 by Sherri Winston

Little, Brown and Company

Hachette Book Group
1290 Avenue of the Americas, New York, NY 10104
Visit us at lb-kids.com

Little, Brown and Company is a division of Hachette Book Group, Inc.
The Little, Brown name and logo are trademarks of Hachette Book Group, Inc.

The publisher is not responsible for websites (or their content)
that are not owned by the publisher.

First Paperback Edition: August 2016
First published in hardcover in November 2015 by Little, Brown and Company

The Library of Congress has cataloged the hardcover edition as follows:

Winston, Sherri, author.
President of the whole sixth grade / Sherri Winston. — First edition.
pages cm
Sequel to: President of the whole fifth grade.
Summary: Brianna Justice is the president of her Detroit middle school's sixth grade, but she is finding the position a real headache—beside the normal troubles of being in a new school, and the sudden coldness of her old friends, there is a class trip to Washington, D.C. coming up and she needs to figure out how to raise the rest of the money so that the class can go.
ISBN 978-0-316-37723-2 (hardcover) — ISBN 978-0-316-37722-5 (ebook)
1. School field trips—Juvenile fiction.   2. Middle schools—Michigan—Detroit—Juvenile fiction.   3. Money-making projects for children—Juvenile fiction.   4. Friendship—Juvenile fiction.   5. Detroit (Mich.)—Juvenile fiction. [1. School field trips—Fiction.   2. Middle schools—Fiction.   3. Schools—Fiction.   4. Fund raising—Fiction.   5. Friendship—Fiction.   6. African Americans—Fiction.   7. Detroit (Mich.)—Fiction.]   I. Title.
PZ7.W7536Pt 2015
813.6—dc23
[Fic]

2014040299

Paperback ISBN 978-0-316-37724-9

Printing 10, 2020

LSC-C

Printed in the United States of America

President *★* of the *★* Whole <u>Sixth</u> Grade

SHERRI WINSTON

LITTLE, BROWN AND COMPANY
New York   Boston

1

How It All Began...

My name is Brianna Justice.

I am president of the whole sixth grade. If you are thinking that being class president means I'm popular, you're wrong. At least, you would've been—before everything that happened.

The truth is, getting chosen as class president in middle school was NOTHING like it was in elementary.

When we voted for class president in fifth grade, it was a big BIG deal. Win or lose, you knew it meant something—it mattered. Everybody was excited. Hearts were broken. Dreams were realized. It was...*amazing*.

In sixth grade? Yeah, "running" for class president meant having Mr. Galafinkis tap me on the shoulder and ask me to stay after class and fill out some paperwork. I think my only qualification is that I looked least likely to set a fire in the trash can. And I was one of the few kids who was shorter than him.

Anyway, being president of the whole sixth grade was an important job. It didn't matter whether or not you were popular. What mattered was getting the job done.

And the idea of failing started giving me nightmares.

See, every sixth grader at Blueberry Hills Middle School learned about THE BIG class trip to D.C. long before we started middle school. But somehow, despite about seventy-five of us paying our deposits the first week of school, our class was still twenty-five hundred dollars short.

Now it was up to me to turn my classmates into a lean, mean fund-raising machine, otherwise our big trip was not going to happen. And I didn't just *want* us to go—we *had* to go to D.C.

Why I HAD to help the sixth grade get to Washington, D.C.!

1. TO WIN! Each year, the leadership conference has a theme based on government—this year's theme was ancient Rome. We were going to compete with all the other schools to show how much we knew.

2. The most important magazine in the whole wide world, *Executive, Jr.*, was going to be at the conference. The magazine was doing workshops on leadership skills for business success, and offering tips for kids who wanted to start their own businesses. (I WAS ALREADY A BUSINESSWOMAN! And this could help me make my business even BIGGER!)

3. Our school had participated in this trip for twenty years and NO WAY would I be the first president of the whole sixth grade who FAILED. No way!

4. All of the class presidents had to give a speech. The winning speech would earn $1,000 for that school.

5. MOST IMPORTANT: Getting out of town would give me much-needed time with my girls!!!

So, as you can see, I had A LOT riding on this trip. And time was running out.

The whole thing started that one day. The day the museum lady came to our school . . .

2

The Ides of March

Wednesday, October 15

Rome was burning.

That's a metaphor. Maybe with a little hyperbole mixed in. It refers to a massive fire in ancient Rome that destroyed a lot of neighborhoods. It was rumored that this heartless emperor dude, Nero, played the violin while the city burned to the ground.

Living near Detroit, I knew a little bit about fire. Buildings sometimes got torched for no reason, although the city was trying to improve its image. The metaphor, about Rome burning, referred to me. My life. Only in reverse, because my world was burning up while the rest of my classmates fiddled, played, and joked around.

We were studying ancient civilizations, especially Rome, for Civics class. Preparation for learning modern government, our teacher, Mr. Galafinkis, said. We had to keep a journal comparing and contrasting our lives in middle school with life in ancient times.

At first, I thought that assignment was lame. However, it turned out that middle school had a *lot* in common with ancient civilization. Big egos . . . fighting for territory . . . weird clothes. The weak getting thrown to the lions for fun. And lots of **drama.**

Want to know a good vocabulary phrase for Civics?

The Ides of March.

Ancient Romans called the middle of each month the ides. Sometimes, like in the case of Julius Caesar, who found himself dead on March 15, 44 BC, the ides were bad luck. For me, on a particularly disagreeable day in the kingdom of sixth grade, I felt like I was suffering through the Ides of October. And in this case, the ides truly sucked.

Thanks to a laughable shortage of funds in the sixth-grade account, my class presidency was in BIG TROUBLE. Welcome to my world—*The Ides Edition*.

"Aw, girl, we've got plenty of time," cackled some sixth-grade deviant during what could only be described as "The Debacle." DEBACLE—totally a vocabulary word. It means awesomely bad failure.

The Cackler overheard me say how desperate I was to get started with fund-raising. I wanted to smack him in the head with my Civics book. We did not have plenty of time. The clock was ticking. Our trip was scheduled for Monday, December 8. That was less than eight weeks away. Plus, the money was due by December 1.

Which was why we invited today's speaker, a lady from the Henry Ford Museum who specialized in helping kids with fund-raising ideas. She came to help us brainstorm ideas. She was trying to help us raise twenty-five hundred dollars to get to D.C. However, after the way my fellow sixth graders behaved, I bet most of them couldn't even *spell* D.C.

If I could write what I really, REALLY wanted for my journalism assignment, here's what I'd say:

WAS THERE A MOOSE ON THE LOOSE?

(DETROIT)—The sixth graders had their first meeting of the school year today with Ms. Kenya Benson from the Henry Ford Museum in Greenfield Village. The purpose of the meeting was to discuss how to raise the $2,500 needed for our upcoming trip to Washington, D.C.

Sounds simple, right? So simple, even a sixth grader can do it? Apparently not. Like a lot of things in middle school, looks were deceiving.

Civics teacher and class trip advisor Mr. Galafinkis arranged for the students to meet with Ms. Benson because she specializes in school fund-raisers. But she said only a few words before the whole meeting got out of hand.

Maybe it was the macaroni surprise in the cafeteria. Maybe cafeteria food does something to turn students into mutants. Or maybe there's

(continued)

something to the rumor about that whole zombie virus thing. Maybe middle school water is filled with soul-sucking pathogens that turn perfectly decent sixth graders into soulless flesh-eaters who need to infect others in order to fit in.

Because something like that is the only explanation for what happened next. See, when the nice museum representative began speaking, a strange noise started coming from the back of the room. It was kind of a squawk and kind of a honk. It sounded like a moose. With a head cold.

Soon the sickly moose sounds were coming from everywhere, until finally the nice museum lady was eyeing the door, patting me on the shoulder, and saying, "Good luck!" She said it the same way she might say it to an astronaut being sent onto a cold, deadly planet to tame a nest of gooey aliens determined to destroy Earth.

Whatever possessed the kids to make the moose sounds, one thing is clear—THEY SUCK!

Thank you and leave me alone.

My three best friends and I had been so psyched about starting middle school. But then we got here and the whole world fell apart. Hyperbole again? Okay... maybe not the WHOLE-whole world fell apart. Sure was starting to feel that way, though.

The four of us were used to being in class together, eating lunch together, going to recess together. Now Becks and I were in honors classes, which were mostly in their own hall, unfortunately nicknamed "Lame Land" by the rest of the school. And the school was so big that even after six weeks, I *still* got lost.

That wasn't the worst part, though. Getting lost I could manage. It was the weirdness that drove me insane. Sometimes sixth grade felt so stupid I just wanted to punch myself in the face. Like, repeatedly!

Take Becks, my very best friend in the world. She used to wash her hands all the time because she was obsessed with germs. A pure hypochondriac—which means someone always afraid of getting sick. Now all she could talk about was wanting a boyfriend and wondering what it was like to get kissed.

And sweet, sweet Sara. It was as if every day was costume day. She said she was "expressing herself

10

through the way she dressed." Two weeks into school, she started wearing only jeans and graphic tees. Now she was into pink. Like, *really* into pink. Seriously? *Seriously?*

As if that wasn't crazy enough, there was the whole size thing. In fifth grade, I was considered short. Okay, maybe I wasn't just *considered* short. I was—*am*—short. Or, excuse me, "vertically challenged." Anyway, so what? I could take a joke—I even had a T-shirt that said FUN SIZE. But in middle school, it was hard to just laugh it off.

Every day, and I do mean every single day, I got called everything from Baby to Itty-Bit. Random kids I barely knew would sometimes swoop me off my feet and twirl me around. Worse, Becks started doing it, too.

In grade school I was a lion. I roared like a lion. Queen of the jungle! However, with each passing day of middle school, I was more ly-ing than lion.

Why all the lying? Because middle school was the Land of Fake-Believe. Nobody in that place was honest about who they were or how they felt. Everything was some big fake-out. I told myself I was better than that. I didn't have to fake about anything.

At least, that was what I wanted to believe. It started small. Little lies, like laughing along with my friends even though I thought their video or Facebook post or whatever really wasn't all that funny.

Or pretending to be interested when everybody around me talked about getting with this boy or that girl, hundred-dollar sneakers, or who was kind of ratchet. Trust me, ratchet—not good.

Pretty soon I was faking more and more. Like, I faked that it didn't bother me that Sara and Becks seemed to be drifting away.

And I faked that I was cool with getting swooped around and called Baby Smurf. And when somebody fake-coughed and called me Nerd Girl or Dorkopolis just because I took honors classes, I faked like I didn't even care.

See what I mean? That was a lot of faking. I was getting pretty unhappy, but did I tell the truth and admit it? No! It was like admitting how I felt would make me look like even more of a loser.

When I climbed aboard the big, shuddering school bus after that dismal meeting, I was about done with middle school. I wondered if I could move into the Michigan woods and be homeschooled by wolves. (Well, since it was Michigan, maybe I could be schooled by Wolverines.) The bus shook again and my stomach grumbled. School buses were the worst. Especially when the driver looked at us like we were serial killers.

A lot of my classmates dressed like clones of their fave online stars. Girls with T-shirts pulled tight and held in back with rubber bands; boys wearing gym shoes that cost more than Daddy's car payment.

Kids pushed to get to their favorite seats. And as usual, everyone was being mega loud.

Sara handed me my clipboard and squeezed my shoulder.

Becks whispered, "Don't worry, Bree-Bree. It's just your first meeting with them. A lot of kids don't even know you yet."

Today's meeting was the first time a lot of the sixth grade had laid eyes on me. It had not gone as I'd diagrammed it on my trusty clipboard.

I plopped onto the bus seat and slid over to the window. Sara sat down beside me and immediately began whispering across the aisle to Becks about some boy who was "beyond cute." I couldn't help wondering where, exactly, on the map "beyond cute" was. I mean, did you take a right just past Handsome and go three blocks, crossing the Bridge of Attractiveness? I'm just saying.

Lauren sat in front of me, turned in her seat, and scoped out the action up and down the aisles. "Did you know that the world record for the largest bubble gum bubble is twenty inches in diameter?" She giggled. Then she blew a huge bubble and cracked it.

I couldn't help smiling at her. Lauren had always liked world records. At least she hadn't gone totally bonkers the way Sara and Becks had.

When did two of my best friends decide to become boy-crazed loonies? Was I next, destined to be the costar in their horror movie, *Creature from the Boy-Crazy Lagoon!*?

"Your friend," Sara said, knocking me out of my deep thoughts. I looked up and another kid from our elementary days moved into view. Raymond Wetzel. Nicknamed Weasel. His mother owned Wetzel's Bakery, where I worked as a cupcake chef. My whole life, all I'd wanted to do was be a millionaire cupcake baker.

Okay, maybe not my whole life. It might've only been since fourth grade. Still...

Weasel was a funny-looking kid who made weirdness a hobby. But somehow we'd become sort of friends. He raised his hand to wave. Before he had a chance to say a word to us, though, a large chunk of balled-up paper came sailing through the air.

PLUNK! Hit him right in his face. Ouch.

My mouth fell open. Several kids laughed and pointed.

I waited to see what Weasel would do, but he just looked at me, shrugged, then turned and trudged toward the front of the bus. Behind us, I could hear laughing, and one voice saying, "Yeah, you take yo' geeky behind back to the front!"

Between the moose calls, crazy moos, and being humiliated in front of the museum lady, I had had enough. I stomped into the aisle, Sara tugging at my sleeve.

I didn't recognize the paper-ball thrower, but it didn't matter. Somebody needed to set these kids straight.

"Hey!" I yelled. "Why don't you grow up?"

The boy sneered. He had mean, beady eyes and wore the kind of expression that said he was no stranger to detention.

"Awwww, shut up . . . *Jelly Bean*!" he said.

That was followed by a chorus of laughter. Sara gasped, Becks's eyes got huge behind her glasses, and Lauren immediately jumped to her feet.

Jelly Bean. Just because some eighth grader had decided my electric-blue pants and candy-apple-red Converse were too bright and said, "Dang, girl! You look like a big jelly bean," now it was a thing. I'm sure people thought if they said it, I was supposed to be all embarrassed.

Well, I had a surprise waiting for my would-be tormentors. The next person to try to shame me with that stupid nickname was going to learn a thing or two about Brianna Diane Justice.

I removed a ginormous plastic bag filled with jelly beans from my backpack. I opened it and scooped a handful into my mouth.

I chomped them.

I grinned with multicolored globs of jelly-bean goo stuck in my teeth like a psycho jelly-bean fiend.

My heart hammered in my chest. I didn't really *want* to be a psycho jelly-bean fiend, but, see, that was the thing about middle school. Sometimes it made you do stuff that you just couldn't explain. When I'd finally swallowed enough sugary candy not to choke, I said:

"Maybe I do dress like a jelly bean, but I can always buy new clothes. I know you're not trying to talk about how anybody looks! Looking like what would happen if Frankenstein and Bigfoot had a baby!" The back of the bus erupted into laughter.

With way more confidence than I felt, I spun around, flinging the zippered plastic bag like some sort of crazy flag.

A stampede of jelly-bean-hungry sugar freaks drowned out the "oh snap" and "man, she told you" chorus that filled the air.

I slumped back against my seat. I thought shutting down a bully would make me feel better. It kinda did, but it also didn't. The bus driver yelled for everyone to be quiet. Then the old yellow school bus staggered into traffic.

Beyond the window, trees rushed past. Their giant green Afros of summer leaves had transformed into an array of dappled red and gold 'dos. As the bus's tires flung gravel and grit across the cement road beneath us, Sara whispered, "Brianna, you're *soooooo* brave."

I wanted to believe her. I really did. But I was afraid that the truth was, I was just a much better faker than she knew. Maybe I was the biggest fake of all.

Civics Journal
Ancient Rome and Middle School

Dear Journal,

Mr. Galafinkis has us keeping a journal on ancient Rome. He says if we can relate what we learn to our lives, we'll really remember it, not just memorize it for tests and quizzes.

Based on today, how can I compare my life to what we've been studying?

Ancient Rome was a caste society. Which means people were treated differently based on whether they were citizens, noncitizens, or slaves. Commoners were called plebeians.

Middle school is divided into sixth, seventh, and eighth grades. Sixth graders are treated like plebeians. We compete just to be commoners. The lowest members of society.

Well, technically, slaves would have been the lowest. But they didn't get to vote or have a voice. I wonder if plebeians ever made moose sounds while a senator was speaking to them. Probably the Romans would feed the rude plebeians to the lions.

I wonder if the Detroit Zoo has any lions to loan to the leader of the plebeians...

3

Pandora's Box

Friday, October 17

The world looked upside down.

Maybe because I was standing on my hands.

I needed to figure out how we were going to raise twenty-five hundred dollars.

Today was a teacher workday, so, thank goodness, no school. I'd invited my friends over to sample a few new cupcake recipes I was working on. Also, we were supposed to discuss fund-raising for D.C.

"Bree, how long are you going to stand on your hands? You know that freaks me out!" said Sara. Then she snapped a selfie with her phone.

"Being upside down helps me think," I said.

"I heard it promotes hair growth," said Becks, also holding her phone. But she wasn't taking pictures, just texting. "Not that you need your hair to grow any more."

I shook my head and heard Becks make a sound between a laugh and a snort. My hair, when I was upright, hung past my shoulders. Sometimes, if I fluffed it out, it looked like it was swallowing me. Cool, right? Grandpa said when it was like that, I looked like Cousin It. Hmm...

Lauren, whose blond ponytail swished when she walked, knelt in front of the oven and asked, "How much longer until this batch is finished?"

"About two minutes," I answered.

"You're such a great cook, Brianna!" she said.

"Tell that to my Home Ec teacher. I'm struggling to get even a B in that class," I said.

"You don't have an A in Home Ec??" Sara asked, shocked. "That's rough."

I nodded.

It felt like the scent of cake flour and chocolate enveloped the whole wide world. My world, at least.

We'd spent a lot of time in here together over the

years. And we'd eaten a lot of cupcakes. We'd started talking about the D.C. trip right here, actually, gushing about how amazing it was going to be.

"D.C. is going to be *craaaaaaaay-zeeeee*!" Becks said. "We should definitely go to the White House." I thought that was a great idea, but wasn't sure why she giggled when she said it. And she and Sara shared this... *look* before slapping high fives.

"Why? What's so funny?" I asked.

Lauren said, "Yeah, I mean, going to the White House sounds amazing. But why're you laughing?"

"Becks wants to go so she can meet her boo! The First Nephew. Code Name: Neptune. He is so *foin*!" said Sara.

Foin. Since sixth grade started—a whole six weeks ago—Sara had upped her urban slang. It was like she'd downloaded some kind of app for street cred and was determined to get her money's worth.

"Who?" asked Lauren.

Becks tapped on her phone. "Him!" She showed us a photo of a kid with hair so long and curly that it covered his eyes. He was standing on a diving board. Wearing a pair of those teeny-tiny swim trunks.

Lauren blushed and I felt uncomfortable. But Becks said, "He doesn't know it yet, but one day he's going to marry me."

"And I'm going to be the bridesmaid, and the wedding will be held poolside!" Sara giggled, and this time she and Becks fist-bumped. I gave them a look like *Really?* If you get the chance to go to the White House, your first quest would be to trap the poor First Nephew kid in a broom closet?

"Seriously, I can't wait 'til we go to D.C.," Sara said. I went back into a handstand. My hair fell in my face and covered my eyes.

Sara went on, "At least in D.C., I won't have to deal with my parents."

No one said anything. Sara's parents were getting a divorce. Okay, that was really crummy, right? But lately, Sara was finding a way to work it into EVERY conversation. We'd be, like, "Broccoli is my favorite vegetable," and she'd be all, like, "We used to eat broccoli all the time, before my dad left...." When she brought it up, I had to count to ten or a million to keep from just going off!

Becks glanced up from her texting and said, "Forget D.C. I can't wait 'til we go shopping on Black Friday."

"Christmas shopping plans already?" said Lauren.

"Mom said I can't withdraw money from my savings account 'til then," Becks huffed.

"Me, too," said Sara. "With her and Dad splitting, she says money is tight."

One thousand one, one thousand two, one thousand three...

Sara's mom worked at a bank. The four of us had been saving our money, going to the bank every Saturday to make deposits. We used to call ourselves the Woodhull Society. We got the name from the first female presidential candidate, Victoria Woodhull. She was also into finances and saving. I wrote a research paper on her in fifth grade. Anyway, saving used to be a big thing for us.

Now Becks and Sara seemed to want to make more deposits at the mall than at the bank. Another change I didn't like.

Sara and Becks launched into a discussion about fashion, then went all gaga over Prya and Paisley.

Who are Prya and Paisley, you ask?

Paisley (PĀZ-lē)—*A troll doll in designer clothes. Laughs at her own jokes and wears too much body* *spray, so she smells like a garden exploded in her underwear. A poor student, grade-wise, yet she always has something to say.*

Prya (PRĒ-ah)—*See above. Plus, she looks like she just discovered a turd in her lunch box; so her nose is always scrunched up. When she laughs, she collapses in on herself as though jokes have the power to dissolve her spine.*

"You can't really want to hang out with those girls, right?"

Sara looked at me and said that the Peas were known for their fashion sense. (Prya and Paisley were called that—the Peas. Ugh, right?) I thought they were known for not having a whole *lot* of sense, but I kept it to myself.

Becks looked up from her texting and said, "Maybe you should try to get to know them, Bree. You don't have to be so judgmental all the time."

"I am not judgmental! And no thank you to getting to know them!" I answered. "They're mean and cliquish and rude."

Becks went back to texting. Over her shoulder, she said, "Anyway, don't worry about the fund-raising. We'll get it done!"

"Unless she falls and breaks her neck first. Brianna, stand up. You're freaking me out!" said Sara. *Snap, snap!* The phone's camera whirred.

"Know what freaks me out? The fact that you're dressed like one of those dolls our moms wouldn't let us play with when we were little because they looked too . . . what was the word your mom used, Becks?"

"*Provocative,*" she said, taking a hit off her inhaler. Becks's asthma was legendary.

Then we cracked on her a little. I said she looked like she'd been attacked by a pop princess.

"No!" said Lauren. "More like she got beat up by a rogue band of Barbies and forced into one of their special little closets!"

We all hooted.

Sara said, "Ha-ha. Very funny. So? Pink is my new color. It's extra-girlie, like me. And Brianna, I love you, but you're not exactly a fashionista."

Now they were laughing again, only this time at

27

me. All good, I could take it. I shifted my weight from one hand to the other.

Becks said, "*Jelly bean* is not a fashion statement." Okay...

Just then, the timer beeped. I flipped down from the wall. One of Katy's scabby cats wandered into the kitchen and I quickly chased it out. My sister was in high school. She was one of those girls who wanted to save every stray animal on the planet.

"Nobody cared about how bright my clothes were when we were in elementary," I said, brushing cat hair off my hands and rinsing them in the sink. Using an oven mitt, I took out the cupcakes and scooped batter into another muffin tin while the hot ones cooled.

Becks scooted over to let me onto the stool beside her at the kitchen island. "Bree, we're not in elementary anymore. This is the big time. Middle school. I might not be dressed in head-to-toe pink like Sara, but, well, sometimes I think about changing—"

"We don't need to change!" I cut her off.

Sara was busy posing. *Snap! Snap! Snap!* Three selfies in a row, a personal best. She said, "Well, I like my new style."

"I think you look like a puffball!"

We all turned around to see my cousin, Liam. He was five years old, wearing a plaid hunter's shirt, his face round as a chocolate moon pie. Lauren and I were cracking up. He was right. With those ridiculous pink boots and that fuzzy pale pink hat, Sara did look kinda like a puffball. A skinny puffball.

Becks rolled her eyes. "All I know is, once I lose about twenty pounds, I'm buying a whole new wardrobe. I think I can lose that much between now and the time we go shopping."

I said, "God, Becks! Would you please stop all this 'I gotta lose twenty pounds' foolishness? Besides, I read that trying to lose more than two pounds a week is, like, dangerous."

Becks was not having it. She said, "Being fat is dangerous, too. Bree, you just don't get it! You're teeny-tiny."

I shot back, "In fifth grade you never worried about your weight."

Her eyes got big and her expression grew dark. She was almost shouting. "I DID TOO CARE! I cared about my weight, I just didn't say anything!"

I turned back to her. "You were fine then, you're fine now. Why do you need to lose weight anyway?"

Sara cut in, "Becks has a crush on Bakari Jones. He's in the band."

I said, "You mean that little dude who thinks he's funny?"

"He is funny. And cute!" Becks said. We sat in silence for a few seconds, letting Becks get a hold of herself. She sucked in a deep breath and blew it out. After a few more seconds, she slid off the barstool.

She said, "I just don't want to be the fat girl. I mean, look at this!" She plastered the front of her shirt over her stomach. Okay, I admit, the shirt was too tight. Actually, I had noticed she'd been wearing all her clothes tighter.

"Stop that! You wouldn't have that problem if you just wore bigger shirts," I said.

"Oh, please, Brianna. You... you just don't understand what it's like to be heavy."

I countered, "Becks, you're not—"

But she cut me off. And the change in her tone was so hard and loud, even the old clock on the stove seemed to freeze.

"Brianna, people at school, even the ones who mess with you about dressing too bright like a jelly bean or whatever, they think you're cute. They say, 'Brianna Justice? You mean the cute girl with all the hair?' Or they'll say, 'She's so adorable.' That's what people say about you behind your back. You know what people say about me?

"They say, 'That's Rebecca. No, not Rebecca Robinson. The other one. The fat one. The one who hangs around with the girl in pink and the cute little one with the clipboard who bosses everybody around!' It is no fun to have people say that kind of thing to your face, Brianna. That's why I'm getting rid of this belly."

We all stared in horrible silence as she reached down and grabbed the soft fluff of her stomach, the part that squished over the top of her too-tight jeans. My mouth was completely dry. I'd never seen Becks so angry. I took a breath. In my mind, I said, *Be easy, Brianna!* I figured being a leader meant keeping your cool, you know. *Just, be easy.*

"That sure is a big belly!" Liam said.

We gasped. Not because he was wrong, but, well, even before this meltdown, we'd fallen into a pattern with Becks. She'd say something mean about how her body looked and the rest of us would spend the next half hour trying to convince her she was wrong.

Apparently, five-year-olds didn't understand the subtlety of middle school insanity.

"Well, if you're really serious, maybe you could come work out with me and my mom. You know, I go to the gym with her on the weekends," I said.

For some bizarre reason, I felt responsible, like I had single-handedly given Becks unwanted belly fat, and then, like a maniac, went around shrinking her pants and tops so she'd feel extra-uncomfortable.

She shook her head. "Never mind, Bree. I'm going to lose weight on my own. You'll see."

I shooed Liam away and went back to my baking.

With a batch of cupcakes cooling and another ready to go into the oven, I joined everybody at the counter.

"Um, fund-raising?" Lauren prompted again, crossing her arms.

I said, "Yes, about fund-raising. Anybody ever hear of Torture the Teacher?"

Torture the Teacher was just one of the fund-raising ideas I'd found on the Internet. You get a bunch of teachers to agree to different types of "torture." Goofy stuff like wearing their clothes inside out, or dressing like the '80s, stuff like that. You charge a dollar per ticket and you get kids to buy chances to use them to vote on the teacher they'd like "tortured." The teacher with the most votes wins. Or, actually, loses.

Sara said, "Torture sounds kinda mean, Bree. What if we get in trouble?"

"Oh, Sara," I said. "They'd be agreeing to the torture. See? No one is going to get into trouble."

She said, "Well, saaaaaaaaar-reeeeeeeee! I didn't get it at first. I'm not in honors like you and Becks."

Becks, glancing up from her text-a-thon, snorted. "Honors is not all it's cracked up to be. It ain't all that."

I rolled my eyes so hard I almost saw the future. Becks never used to use poor grammar, like *ain't*. She was really changing.

So it went back and forth like that. Eventually, they all agreed the fund-raiser sounded like a good idea. We talked about a few others that they liked, too. I took notes on my trusty clipboard.

"Brianna, you know, if you got an iPad or something, you could get an app that acts like a clipboard to keep up with your ideas," Sara said. "You've had that thing since we were in second grade. Remember the time you made those cakes and got in trouble for selling them at recess?"

Lauren was snorting, she was laughing so hard. "Bree, that was so funny. You made these little cakes in your Easy-Bake Oven and brought them to school and sold them. And you used that thing to keep track of just how many you sold. How much money did you make selling that stuff?"

"Eight dollars and twenty-eight cents! And yes, this is the same clipboard. It's my lucky clipboard. Why do I need to change? I used it to calculate the first money I earned, and I plan to use it when I calculate my first million."

"Yeah, we all know you hate change almost as much as you *loooooove* money," Becks said.

I said, "Well, we all like saving money."

"Not as much as you," Becks grunted.

"What is that supposed to mean?" I crossed arms over my chest. My head got to swiveling and I waved my finger around as I talked. "Last year all of us cared about our savings accounts. All of us went to the bank together and made deposits. It's only been since the start of the school year that *some of us* have decided to act all brand-*new* and stop meeting up for our Victoria Woodhull Society meetings!"

"Okay, girls, let's not fight," Sara jumped in. She was always playing peacemaker. I wondered if that fit in with her new, ultra-girlie personality. "Bree, Becks is just saying we all know that money is, like, the most important thing to you."

For some reason, her saying that stung. Like I had been hit in the face with a dodgeball. Money would never be more important to me than my friends. They knew that, right?

I sighed. Part of me had hoped we could talk. Really talk. About middle school and feeling weird and fake. Once upon a time, our futures were all set. We'd planned them out—together. I just wanted to remind them of that without sounding lame.

But I couldn't help myself. When I reminded them of our lifelong plans—of me becoming a cupcake-baking millionaire; Becks, a famous author; Sara, an Olympic horseback rider; and Lauren, a famous Hollywood stunt-woman—Becks and Sara shared another one of their looks.

Sara came over and gave me a hug. Random hugs were a *thing* in middle school. Girls hugged all the time, some clinging to each other like life rafts, some constantly offering or receiving piggyback rides. Becks tried to get me to ride on her back once, but I told her I'd rather shave my head and donate my savings to a school that taught bullies how to steal lunch money.

Sara sighed. "Oh, Bree, that's what we wanted when we were little. I mean, when we came up with those futures, we were just kids."

Seriously? "Sara! We were talking about this stuff, like, two months ago. Remember? We were down at the stables where your family keeps its horses. You were with Buttercup."

She made a face and sighed extra-dramatically. "Well, you know, that was before I found out my parents were getting divorced. We can't keep the horses anymore," she said, grabbing her phone and moving around the kitchen taking pictures of herself.

"No biggie. I think I'd outgrown the horses, anyway." *Snap! Snap! Snap! Snap! Snap! Snap! Snap!*

And there it was. The fakery. She was telling a big, fat lie. I knew it. She knew it. And she had to know we all knew it. Why was it so hard to just admit she was sad? Why was it getting so hard for any of us to say what we were really feeling?

The timer on the oven beeped again and I removed the second batch. We all took turns using my pastry bag to squeeze frosting designs onto the already-cooled cupcakes. Everyone sampled except Becks. The guilty feeling I'd had earlier about her weight came back. She normally loved my cupcakes. Now I really did wonder if she blamed me for some of her weight gain.

Becks said she wasn't hungry. No one tried to convince her otherwise.

We didn't say much else. Maybe we'd all had enough fakery for one day.

Civics Journal
Ancient Rome and Middle School

Mr. Galafinkis told us that myths and stuff like that were real popular in ancient Rome. I'd heard this expression about "opening Pandora's box" before, but I never knew what it meant. He said it came from the Greeks, but during the time of ancient Rome, they created their own version. He said the ancient Romans were always borrowing from the Greeks and not giving them credit. Sorta like hip-hop artists are always stealing from classic R&B singers and never giving them their due. (At least, that's what Grandpa says.)

So, back to Pandora's box. Mr. G. said this Greek god, Zeus, gave his daughter Pandora a jar or box or whatever as a wedding present. He told her to never open it. Well, of course she did, and all the evils of the world flew out. Mr. G. says when people think of Pandora's box, they're looking at how something seemingly innocent, like opening a box, can turn into a big deal, like, you know, unleashing evil on the whole world.

So, I couldn't help thinking about the latest baking session in my kitchen. It started off innocently enough. But after the way Becks flew off the handle about me not understanding what it was like to be fat, and Sara practically laughing in my face about my so-called style, I wondered if I had opened my own Pandora's box. Mr. G. said after all the world's evils flew out, one tiny bug with a smiling face came out. It was hope. Was there still hope for us as best friends?

4

The Republic of Rome

Monday, October 20

If I thought life would be simple once we came up with fund-raising ideas for D.C., I was tragically mistaken.

My morning started at five a.m., at Wetzel's Bakery.

Three or four days a week, Grandpa drove me there to bake cupcakes. Luckily, Grandpa lived with us now. He said old people don't sleep through the night, so he was up at that time of day anyway. He usually came into the bakery for coffee, and sometimes he sat around chatting up a few of the older dudes who worked there.

I got my cupcakes going, made my frosting, and whipped up a batch of breakfast muffins—banana walnut and apple raisin.

On a normal school day, I stayed until seven thirty. Then Weasel and I would walk to the bus stop together. But since the principal asked all class presidents, club presidents, and anyone else involved in a "leadership capacity" to meet at his office at seven a.m., Grandpa came back to give me a ride.

When I got to school, I totally had a plan. I was going to rock it with the sixth graders today. My clipboard rested safely in my book bag, and my plan relied on me getting them to do what I wanted them to do.

Assistant Principal Snidely scowled when I passed his office. "You're late, Miss Justice."

I apologized and he pointed down the hall to a conference room, eyeing me like I'd been caught puffing an electronic cigarette in the girls' bathroom. Principal Striker had his back to me when I entered. He was standing at a table pouring coffee. One quick look around the room told me I wasn't late after all. The meeting hadn't started.

When I went over to get a cup of coffee, I received my second scowl of the morning. (A two-scowl morning. Should've been a sign.)

"Do your parents allow you to drink coffee?" the principal asked. He was a tall man with hands the size of lunch boxes. It was rumored that he'd paid his way through the University of Florida by wrestling alligators.

"As long as I don't do it every day, it's cool," I said, and he filled my cup—halfway, at least.

I saw his eyes stray from the tray of stale bagels on the oak-grain table to the Wetzel's Bakery bag I was carrying.

"Muffins," I said. "Would you like one?"

When I opened the bag, his dark brown eyes went soft, like he'd just seen the most amazing Cadillac in the world. (This was Detroit. Grown men have been known to get misty-eyed over the beauty of a Caddie.)

I passed the bag around the conference table, and the muffins vanished faster than a cheater's palm during a chapter test. Braxton Brattley, president of the seventh grade, glared at me, which made the whole muffin experience even more delightful.

Braxton was a first-rate fungus, but a second-rate human being. Shaped like an evil rectangle with a piggish little nose, he'd been on my case since the day Mr. Galafinkis picked me to be president. Kept saying how his brother would be a better president and how he'd been hoping the two of them could be in charge of sixth and seventh grade at the same time.

Over the next forty-five minutes, Principal Striker discussed how he expected all of us to conduct ourselves as leaders in the school and as positive representatives in the community. He also told us that he'd need to approve all fund-raising events in advance.

His voice boomed in a thick baritone and his broad smile revealed two front teeth that had a small gap in between. "And as most of you may know," he added, "many of us are looking forward to the big Old-School Jam concert taking place November twenty-second, so be careful picking dates for your events. You don't want to book an event on a date when your chaperones have plans of their own!"

I laughed to myself, thinking about how my parents were already excited about the Old-School concert. Music that existed back in the day before the Internet or iPods.

After the meeting ended, we all hung around the front office until morning announcements. Each class president told his or her class during which period they'd have their assembly. When it was my turn, I told the sixth graders when we'd meet, then I told them not to worry.

"We may have gotten off to a rough start," I said, trying to sound confident, "but trust me, I've got some ideas that'll make us enough money for our trip. Trust me!"

As soon as I got to the outer hall, my favorite seventh-grade bully blocked my path. "I saw you in there, Brianna Justice. With your little muffins!" said Braxton Brattley. Every time he talked, he made little snort sounds.

"Um, yeah. I'm not invisible, Braxton. Everybody in the room saw me. My muffins, too."

I tried going around him, but he moved over and blocked me again.

"Being a giant suck-up to Principal Striker won't help you." *Snort!* "You're still going down. You wait!"

"Do you hear yourself? You need a big cup of get-over-yourself. The sixth grade does not need you. Now GET OUT OF MY WAY!"

This time he stepped aside, but not before saying, "*Everybody* knows how badly your first meeting went, Justice. Don't be stupid. I'll bet you don't even have any ideas." *Snort! Snort! Snort!*

I spun around so fast his little piggy nose was still twitching. "Look, not that it's any of your business, but we came up with some *great* ideas. We're doing a Teacher Torture. We're also doing a bake sale, because

I am a professional baker, Braxton. And we're doing 'A Night of Stars,'" I said, recalling Sara's idea to host a talent night that included a red carpet and photos with the "stars" of the show.

Braxton looked at me with a cockeyed gaze. His thin, wormy lips tried to smile. On him, smiles were not a good look.

The second bell was ringing, and I had to get all the way to the honors hall. I saluted him as I dashed off to my Civics class, feeling really good.

I☆I☆I☆I

When I walked into Mr. G.'s classroom, I could see he was all business. I slipped into my seat and began copying the notes on the board.

After skimming his roll book, he asked, "Who here remembers our discussion on the Twelve Tables and what they meant in ancient Rome?"

Clearly, he wasn't in the mood for any foolishness. I decided it'd be best to look like I was paying attention. So I raised my hand.

When Mr. G. nodded at me, I explained what I

remembered about the lesson. How the Twelve Tables referred to the bronze tablets where all the rules and laws of Roman society were chiseled. Once the Romans got rid of their king and became a republic—a government where citizens can elect their representatives—writing down the laws was a way to show they applied to everyone from the upper crust to the plebeians.

Mr. G. grinned, and I exhaled, thankful I'd gotten it right. Then, of course, he had to go and spoil it with an assignment.

"Students, in your journals on ancient Rome, I'd like you to create your own Twelve Tables. Only, I want you to come up with the Twelve Laws of Middle School. By the end of the marking period, I want to see what you believe the laws of this school are—or should be."

I☆I☆I☆I

Mrs. Galafinkis was Mr. G.'s wife. She could be just as intense as he was, but she was also just as good. Our class, Beginning Journalism, was mostly sixth and seventh graders. Much to my surprise, I loved it.

Every day we read stories from the paper and

discussed them. Like real human beings. My auntie Tina worked for the *Detroit Free Press*, so I grew up reading the paper. But reading it with the class felt different. More adult.

Using the iPads that Mrs. G. had available for each student, we scrolled through the *Detroit Free Press* article we were instructed to read. It was about the Oakland County sheriff's office arresting a woman who was homeless and living in her car with her two kids. She had a job interview and left the kids—one was six and the other one was three—all alone. When she came out of the interview, they arrested her for child neglect.

"So, reporters, how do you feel about the story?" Mrs. G. said.

The way she peered at us through her glasses made us feel important. Also, she was only a little bit taller than me, which officially made her the shortest teacher at school.

Anyway, once we read through the article, hands immediately went up. Several kids believed that the police were being cruel, arresting a homeless woman.

I shoved my hand into the air. "Um, what were

they supposed to do? She left them in a car. Anything could've happened!"

Now several pairs of eyes turned on me. "You're as bad as the cops!" said one kid. Several others started talking. Lots of heads bobbed in agreement.

But Mrs. G. said, "Let Brianna make her point."

I blew aside a wisp of hair from my messy top-knot. "Look," I said, "it's too bad the lady is homeless or whatever. But wrong is wrong. That's why we have rules. Laws. You can't go around leaving little kids alone like that. It's dangerous. What if some creepy guy had seen those kids by themselves?"

Another girl clearly disagreed. "No! You're wrong. Look around. How many people in Detroit are homeless? How many houses are abandoned? It's on the news all the time. You're wrong, and so is the sheriff's department."

Then the chant began.

"Point-counterpoint! Point-counterpoint! Point-counterpoint!" and on and on, until Mrs. G. smiled and raised her hand, putting a stop to it. It was settled. I would write a counterpoint essay—the opposite opinion of the girl scowling at me.

I wasn't worried. Mine would be better. Because I was right.

Click, a kid in the class, came over to my desk. Julio Ramon Garcia, aka Click, was a quiet kid who liked making little movies and building stuff with Legos. He'd been carrying Lego pieces around with him since kindergarten. When he wanted to really make a point, he'd click the pieces together. You know? For emphasis.

"What?" I said. He grinned. Bounced his eyebrows up and down. *Click-click!* went the pieces.?

I really liked Click. He was so quiet, but when you got to know him, he was like this creative genius.

"You think we should make a mini-movie about the point-counterpoint?"

Click. Click. Click.

Every week he and I worked on a mini-movie as part of our journalism assignment. We did something called stop-motion, where we took like a gazillion photos, moving the LEGO pieces one foot after the other, snapping each photo, then putting them all together. Click usually edited the final project, but I was trying to learn to do more of it. Then Mrs. G. showed the mini-movies on Fridays during the morning news show. Kids loved 'em.

The bell rang, and Click was still at my desk when Sara came crashing into the room.

"Excuse me!" Mrs. G. said, eyeing Sara.

"I'm sorry!" Sara said. "But this is important...."

She looked frantic. Sara got right in my face, ignoring the monster scowl Mrs. G. was throwing behind her huge glasses.

Sara said, "Brianna! Girl, we've got problems!"

She went on to inform me that Braxton Brattley, that dirty little fungus, had stolen my fund-raising ideas!

The seventh graders had met with President Brattley during third hour and that louse presented MY IDEAS as his own! With the assembly just a few hours away, I was shaking in my bright red Chuck Taylors. Seriously, what was I going to do?

I☆I☆I☆I

I plopped down at center stage in the auditorium, watching the seats fill with sixth graders.

I felt like an army of ants was charging across my intestines. I was pretty sure they were ninja ants. Mean and nasty, with knives.

This was supposed to be a great moment. Me and my good luck clipboard, waiting for a second chance to address my classmates. They were here today because on the morning announcements, I'd promised that I wouldn't let them down. I'd promised that I would deliver a bunch of moneymaking ideas sure to get us all to Washington, D.C.

But I hadn't figured on the Brattley Factor. Dirty little sneak.

I sat bouncing my knees up and down, trying to calm myself. Mr. Galafinkis knelt and touched my shoulder.

"Hey, so you made a mistake. That's how we grow. You're gonna do fine today. Trust me."

My stomach twisted into knots. What *was* I going to do?

My lucky clipboard lay on the floor beside me. I'd already failed once in front of these kids.

Mr. Galafinkis went to the podium. Slowly, I pushed myself up from the floor. Standing in the center of the auditorium stage, I felt like my bright purple pants were starting to glow.

When Mr. G. started talking, most of the students went silent. They looked from him . . . *to me*.

My mouth felt like I'd brushed my teeth with dryer lint. *Nightmare in the Auditorium*, starring Brianna Justice...

Light applause drifted up to the stage. Mr. G. introduced me and I felt a greasy sickness slither into my stomach.

As I began talking, some kids looked really bored. But most looked curious. Almost...interested.

And then I got an idea.

My knees knocked and dots danced before my eyes.

I held up the clipboard.

"When I came to school today, I was all set to share some big ideas I'd brainstormed with my friends. I was so confident. Then..." I drew a deep breath and slowly blew it out.

"...and then, I allowed myself to be tricked by the president of the whole seventh grade. You know him, right? Braxton Brattley!"

The greatest thing in the history of the world happened—they booed Braxton Brattley. *Delicious!*

"Can you believe I fell for something like that? What was I thinking?" Heads nodded. Kids sat forward. They were hooked; they were interested. I explained how he'd taunted me, making me so mad, I told him my ideas.

One boy I didn't recognize yelled, "Aw, girl, you fell for that?"

I said, "I know, right?" shrugging my shoulders.

Then I told them that we—this group of sixth graders—should come up with new fund-raising ideas. Together.

It wasn't long before they were chanting, "SIXTH GRADE RULES! SIXTH GRADE RULES! SIXTH GRADE RULES!"

In the audience, Click sat at the far end of the front row. When I looked over, he waggled one of the LEGOs at me. He smiled, and that made me smile, too.

I asked Lauren, Becks, and Sara to come onto the stage to help me keep track as students started shouting out suggestions.

I wondered if the president of the United States ever got tired of smiling. I was grinning so hard that my cheeks hurt. Jumping around like a talk show host.

Click's hand went into the air. I shushed the room. "Hold on, you guys, I need to hear," I said. Click told me his fund-raising idea. And it was amazing!

He suggested that we provide yard work and garage cleanup services. "Especially in the Oak Woods neighborhood. *Mi abuela*, my grandma, lives in a neighborhood where a lot of, um, older people live. I know she'd pay us to clean out her garage," he said.

"I love that idea, Click," I said. And I meant it.

By the end, we had plenty more excellent ideas. Mr. G. actually high-fived me.

"You did great!" he said.

My entire body buzzed with adrenaline. I couldn't believe it. I'd expected to be booed off the stage. Instead, I'd gotten a bunch of ideas that could raise a lot of money for us.

And I realized that buzzing feeling came from more than getting new ideas, even better ideas than before. I was feeling all jazzed up because...because I had actually motivated the kids to want to work. I'd never really thought about what it was like to motivate someone. It felt really good.

The class meeting gave me a boost. I felt confident we could raise all the money we needed. Still, I couldn't shake the memory of how Braxton Brattley tricked me.

Was he determined to tank the sixth grade?

And if so, what dirty trick would he try next?

Civics Journal
Ancient Rome and Middle School

Middle school and the Republic of Rome really do have something in common.

Ancient Rome was a kingdom before it was a republic—ruled by a king. In a republic, people vote for leadership.

The Romans, especially the lower class, thought it was awesome getting rid of the king. They liked the idea of being able to vote because it meant they would get a chance to be heard.

Okay, so technically we didn't have an election. Mr. G. appointed me to be president. Still, after the assembly today, it was like everybody was involved and they seemed to like it.

I learned today that kids, like Roman citizens, seem to care more when they feel included.

5

Don't Rest on Your Laurels

Tuesday, October 21

The room had a strong scent of plants and leaves.

Of course, that could have been because every place I looked, all I saw were plants—and leaves.

Turns out it was one of Mr. G.'s classic lessons. He asked me and several others to take a seat.

"Quickly, quickly," he called to no one in particular, his eyes focused on the mounds of leaves.

Civics was the last room on the hall in Lame Land, the oldest part of the school. In this section of the building, radiators were loud and windows stretched from floor to ceiling. Outside, the morning sky was watery gray, and damp clumps of leaves swirled across the lawn. Despite the loud radiators and asthmatics, I liked it here.

The honors classes were smaller than classes over in the rest of the school. And over here, teachers talked with us, not just at us. And they listened, too.

Mr. Galafinkis had just dropped a handful of leaves onto his desk when a guidance counselor walked in. The counselor had a girl with him.

New student? If so, I didn't envy her. She was slim, a little taller than me. She had cool red hair and stared out at the room with bright blue eyes.

I had a situation with a new student at my old school. Back in elementary. Didn't work out so well. Still, there was something about this new girl. What really stood out was her attitude. Her expression said, "I'm *not* having it. Whatever *it* is!" She wore all black and her oversized T-shirt had a skull on the front etched in pink rhinestones.

If I'd learned one thing about middle school, it was that new kids were subject to a ridiculous number of rumors. That was just the way it was. By the end of the day, word would probably spread that she was either a vampire or in a motorcycle gang.

Once Mr. G. signed her paperwork and handed

it to the counselor, he looked up and twisted his neck around until he spotted me.

"Brianna, we have a new student. Everyone, this is Scarlett Chastain," he said.

She did a bored sort of eye roll.

"Just call me Red," she said. Her words came out in a drawl.

Mr. G., always flustered and in a hurry, just waved her off. "Yes, dear. Go over there and sit with Miss Justice. She's our class president. Perfect for guiding you through your schedule today. After school I'll have a packet ready for you so you know what's going on."

Red came over and dropped into the empty seat next to me. Oh, my goodness. So much attitude. But for some reason, I wasn't offended at all. A small smile slipped quietly onto my lips. I was tickled. It would be fun to watch her aggravate a bunch of folks around here. Especially the snooty girls who were always ragging on people. Hope she'd eat 'em up!

"Hey," I said. I was being cool and nonchalant— trying to be, at least. She looked like the type who wouldn't appreciate you being all up in her business. I could understand that; I felt the same way.

"Hey, right back at'cha," she said, giving me a sideways grin. "Um, so...the leaves?"

I shrugged. "Every day's a new adventure in Mr. G.'s class."

"Awesome." She pronounced it "ouuuuuuu-some." The way she said it, it did not sound like praise.

After that, Mr. G. got down to business explaining the leaves. "One of the ceremonies at this year's leadership conference involves creating laurel-leaf crowns. Who remembers the purpose of laurel leaves in ancient Roman culture?"

Almost every hand shot up.

Mr. G. said, "Think about your answers before speaking."

Now all the hands were waving, everyone's except mine and the new girl's. Chairs squeaked. Bodies thrashed, hoping to be called on. One thing they didn't tell you was how cutthroat honors classes and advanced programs could be. Everybody wanted to be number one. Maybe it wasn't hard to understand why the rest of the school thought we were lame.

Red leaned over. "And what leadership conference is he talking about?"

"Whole sixth grade, every year for, like, ever, has been participating in this conference in D.C.," I said, acting all nonchalant.

She asked, "So, are you going?"

Her voice was low and a little husky. Her southern accent reminded me of how my grandmother sounded, once upon a time. I liked it.

With a sigh, I said, "I'm in charge of making sure we have enough money to go. And right now..."

All around me, hands waved in the air, eager to answer Mr. G.'s questions, not a care in the world about fund-raising or anything. I'd read the assignment last night but wasn't one of those kids hopping around trying to prove my smartness.

I leaned over instead and whispered, "In ancient Rome, laurel-leaf crowns were worn by important people, like emperors. Or they were worn by military generals after a successful battle." Paused. Then, "So, what's with the accent?"

She shrugged, said, "Can't help it. When you grow up in Dallas, you sound like this."

Mr. G. cleared his throat. "The expression 'Don't rest on your laurels' started in ancient Greece. But remember what we've talked about? The ancient Romans borrowed liberally from the Greeks. Victors of war would wear the laurel-leaf crowns to celebrate." He asked, "So what do victors wearing laurel-leaf crowns have in common with the expression about not resting on one's laurels?"

See? That's what I meant. Over here, in honors, teachers asked for our input instead of just scowling at us. We talked about things.

Mr. G. was sitting on the edge of his desk, arms crossed, waiting. A few hands shot up.

Red looked at me. She said, "If someone tells you not to rest on your laurels, they're saying, *so what* you won the last battle. Don't get too comfortable or you could be toast."

Two or three of my classmates tried answering, hands flapping about. In the end, Mr. G. explained it and said pretty much the same that Red had.

I turned to her and asked, "Know something about not resting on your laurels?"

She whispered back, "Too much, Justice. Too much!"

I☆I☆I☆I

Turns out, Red's schedule was almost identical to mine. When it was time for Journalism, I told her it was my favorite class.

The room was separated into stations. Large circular rugs—red, green, blue—distinguished one area from another. Our seats were at a table that curved into a semicircle. Another identical table was pushed in so that the two halves formed an O. Mrs. G.'s desk sat between one end of the two halves, like a clasp in a bracelet. The desks sat on the blue rug.

"Wow!" said Red. "This place is amazing!"

I gave her a *told-you-so* look.

"Welcome, Miss Scarlett Chastain," Mrs. G. said.

"Red," she corrected. "Call me Red."

"Well, welcome, Red. We're reading the paper this morning. I know that sometimes I let you guys pick what you want. Today, however, there's a particular article I want you to read. I'd like to discuss it. It's the story with the headline that reads BALD AMBITION: TWEENS FACE SUSPENSION FOR HELPING FRIEND.

"Please read through it. Then let's discuss."

We opened the app and began reading. It took only

about five minutes. Then people started saying stuff like, "That's messed up" and "This is so stupid!"

I felt like my chest would explode, I was so angry. Lauren, who'd gotten to class a little late, had just finished reading, too. She looked across the circle at me and I saw that her jaw was clenched. She was mad, too.

Unable to resist, I thrust my hand in the air.

Mrs. G. said, "Brianna, I knew you'd have something on your mind. What do you think of the story?"

"It's the most..." I was sputtering. Took a breath. Tried again. "Mrs. G. Really? Can they really suspend these girls for sticking by their friend Lacy? The girl has cancer. Her friends didn't want her to feel alone, so they shaved their heads so they'd be bald like her. What's the problem?"

Mrs. G. said, "Brianna, calm down. You're yelling."

"Sorry, but I'm just so...so—"

She cut in, "But according to the article, they were warned. The headmaster at their school told them that purposely shaving their heads would be considered a violation of the school's dress code policy."

"Still," I began. "I'm just so..."

"Outraged!" said Red, finishing my thought. Her voice was ragged. Like she was speaking from someplace painful.

"Okay, sorry about yelling," I said, cutting off some other kid who was saying that maybe the school didn't have a choice. I drew a deep breath and glanced back at the photo at the top of the article.

It showed three girls—best friends. The girl who was sick, Lacy, was completely bald. The other two, her friends, had shaved their heads down to fuzz. They'd dyed the thin fluff pale orange, the color used to show support for people with leukemia. Their hair was so short that the orange barely showed, but it was there. And all three girls wore orange ribbons, a show of friendship.

"I think that principal has better things to worry about than girls standing up for one another," I said.

Mrs. G. crossed her arms. I knew this was her point-counterpoint stance.

She said, "But Brianna, their school has a strict policy on appearance and dress. According to the administrator's interpretation of the dress code, the friends, by cutting their hair and dyeing it, violated that policy."

"Okay, I'm usually the one who gets worked up about following the rules..."

"Yeah, like when you wanted to put all the homeless people in jail for being poor!" said a girl I didn't know (and clearly didn't need to meet).

I never even looked her way.

"Anyway, like I was saying," I went on, "I know I'm usually the one trying to follow the rules, but this time they're wrong. Any policy that tries to...I mean, if they won't let friends stick up for one another, it's a bad policy."

For some reason, I felt myself shaking. It was like I was looking at a photo of me and Becks and Sara and Lauren. I glanced over at Red, and her bright blue eyes stared into mine. She bit the corner of her lip, started to say something, then looked away.

The subject seemed to really be bringing her down. It was bringing me down, too. I couldn't stop looking at the photo of the three bald friends. That kind of friendship was worth fighting for. Something like fear burned in my stomach. I knew I had to say something. Do something about this article.

But what was I going to do?

Civics Journal
Ancient Rome and Middle School

That "Don't rest on your laurels" business is no joke. Braxton Brattley made it clear that if I slipped up for just a minute, he'd try to mow me right over. And for what? So his brother can be president? What good would that do Braxton? Still, I need to up my leadership game. Now I know how the Roman senators or emperors felt. Sure can't get any rest when you're protecting your laurels.

6

Spartacus

Tuesday night, October 21

My day kept running through my head. Words crawled over one another and tangled around my brain. When I closed my eyes, I saw those three girls with semi-bald heads, lip-glossed smiles, and eyes fierce, afraid, alive.

Sleep just wasn't happening.

At eleven thirty, I gave up the tossing and turning and went downstairs to the kitchen.

Daddy was still awake. "Hey, Peanut. Why're you up?"

He was making one of his masterpieces. Daddy didn't do simple sandwiches; he made edible art.

"Couldn't fall asleep."

He said, "Perhaps you need a nice light sammy!"

When I was little, he always called sandwiches "sammies." It made me laugh back then—still does.

After pushing a number of ingredients my way—gourmet cheddar cheese from the deli, freshly sliced turkey, a fancy brioche roll—he asked about my day. Daddy worked second shift at the hospital, so I didn't get to see him much anymore during the week. I told him about the laurel leaves, and the aggravating kids at school.

"My Home Ec teacher hates me, too," I said, pouring myself a glass of iced tea. I offered him one, too.

"Get me the lemonade," he said. "And I bet she doesn't hate you."

"I'm pretty sure she does. Daddy, I'm getting a C in her class."

He pointed with his elbow. "Plug in the George Forman, baby. I'm gonna cook this sandwich. A C? That doesn't sound like you."

I told him I knew it didn't sound like me, and he told me I needed to work harder. "Maybe she just wants you to see things her way for a change. You know, you're just like your mother sometimes. You can be a little stubborn."

"Not true!" I said, but laughed.

It was time to change the subject before I got myself into trouble.

So I told him about the new girl whose drawly voice reminded me of Grandma.

He said, "My mama had a world-class drawl." He pushed his thumbs into a head of lettuce, then ripped it apart. Daddy didn't cut lettuce with a knife. He said cutting it made it turn brown faster. I got my love of cooking from him. He taught me how to bake cupcakes and cookies. I loved hanging out with him in the kitchen.

Talking to him about what was on my mind came naturally while he cooked. So it wasn't surprising that before either of us took our first bites I was telling him about the article in the *Free Press*.

When I mentioned the girl with cancer and her friends, what he said knocked me out of my socks. Well, it would have if I'd been wearing socks.

He said, "I know Lacy. She's in the children's ward of our hospital. She's one of my patients."

I was crisscrossing my brioche bread with bright yellow mustard. Several thin slices of turkey clung to one another as I slapped them onto the bun. An idea was forming.

I said, "Daddy, I need your help."

He took a big bite of his creation. "Let me see what I can do," he said.

Wednesday, October 22

After school, Grandpa picked me up. Sara and Becks wanted to know why I wasn't taking the bus, but I just said, "Tell you later!"

I didn't want to tell anyone what I was up to, in case it didn't work out. My heart was beating fast. I bit my lip, tried to play it off like everything was easy-peasy. But I didn't feel easy.

Grandpa pulled into the pickup circle, and the assistant principal waved me along. Didn't want to hold up traffic. The ride didn't take long. Luckily, I'd already written out my questions on my trusty clipboard.

We had to take two elevators and follow a blue

line, then a yellow one. Finally, we rounded a corner, and there they were.

"Here she is!" Daddy said when he saw me.

My stomach twisted into knots. Daddy was standing beside two of the girls from the photo in the *Freep*, and they were all leaning over a third girl in bed.

The three bald friends. This was my idea: Instead of just writing a basic counterpoint, maybe, if I could talk to the actual, real girls, I could write a whole article.

Deep breath!

I said, "Hey, y'all." When I'm nervous, I get all loose with my vowels.

They all said hi.

Daddy introduced me, then totally embarrassed me by telling me to go wash my hands, "thoroughly." Then he explained that because of Lacy's illness, it was easier for her to catch colds and whatnot. He didn't want any middle-school cooties hopping off me and sticking to his patient.

In the bathroom, I took a few more deep breaths. Mrs. G. always said that good journalists speak for their communities. I wanted to speak *for* Lacy and her friends. Which meant first I needed to speak *to* her and her friends.

So we talked. I told them about my school; they told me about theirs. Lacy was seated in a bed that sort of reclined. A tube hung from a bag on a pole and looped up to a spot on her chest. I could see pale stubble on her scalp where her blond hair had been.

Her friends sat on either side of her. I could tell Reagan's hair had been dark. Her head had dark orange stubble. Her eyes were greenish gray. Her smile was so wide that you almost didn't notice the bald head.

Lacy's other friend, Toya, was African American. At first, she looked almost bored, except she wasn't. You could tell. She was fidgety. Angry. She had a little ribbon shaved into the very, very short hair stubble above her right ear. Her face rested on her hand and her elbow was propped on the bed. She was light-skinned, with large brown eyes. If you looked really close, you could see that she was scared. Actually, they all looked a little afraid.

I reread the questions on my clipboard. Mrs. G. had also said that a reporter's story was only as good as her interview. If you don't ask good questions, then when it's time to write the story, you won't have the right kind of information. It was the first time I'd actually interviewed real people who didn't go to our school. I took another deep breath, then got to my list.

I learned Lacy Ann Hart was thirteen. She was an eighth grader at Bloomfield Hills Academy. She was in chorus and orchestra and she liked to draw horses. Only forty-one days earlier, she'd had no idea she had cancer. How scary is that? One day, she's living life all normal and everything. Then, while playing volleyball in gym class, she got hit in the face. Her nose started bleeding and wouldn't stop.

When they took her to the emergency room, Lacy had a lot of tests. That was when they discovered the cancer cells. She had acute lymphoblastic leukemia. Her treatment, called chemotherapy, was like taking a shot that lasted about thirty minutes.

For the second time in two days, I couldn't help remembering my grandmother. She had cancer, too. Her cancer made her so sick that she died. Daddy said cancer didn't always mean dying, though. He said Lacy had an excellent chance at survival. I hoped he was right.

I couldn't imagine this girl dying. She was so young. Like me.

We all talked for a while. Laughed, too. They told

me about Toya being an excellent volleyball player and Reagan singing in chorus with Lacy; I told them about D.C. and how we needed to raise money. I asked all my questions and finished the interview. When I was done, they all hugged me and we took a selfie together. It was like we knew one another, had known one another long before today.

"Thank you for doing this," Reagan said. "I mean...a lot of grown-up reporters have talked to us, but it's nice to talk to someone who understands what it's like being in middle school."

Like a switch being flipped, Toya's laid-back expression suddenly blazed with intensity. Her caramel-colored cheeks flared a hot pink and the teeny-weeny orange 'fro almost glowed as she said, "You know what it means to have friends forever." She clasped Lacy's fingers. "Friends are way more important than hair!"

I worked really hard on my article. When Mrs. G. read it, she decided it was worth more space and attention than just a point-counterpoint that would run on the back page.

She made my article a front-page news feature on the digital and print versions of this week's *Blueberry Chronicle*.

FRIENDS RISK SUSPENSION WITH ACT OF LOVE

Friday, October 24

Friendship is more important than a dress code. When a girl is struggling to survive, and her friends try to help her feel better, nobody should be worried about what they're wearing.

Earlier this week, an article in the *Detroit Free Press* stated that a headmaster in Bloomfield Hills wanted to suspend middle schoolers Toya Mayhew and Reagan Stuart. Why? Just because they shaved their heads to show support for their best friend, Lacy Ann Hart, who had cancer.

Even though the headmaster had warned the girls that they could be suspended for violating the school's dress code policy if they shaved their heads for nonmedical reasons, Reagan and Toya did it anyway. Now they are studying at home while the headmaster decides whether to suspend or expel them.

After I read the article, I knew I had to find out more. My dad works at the same hospital

(continued)

where Lacy gets her cancer treatment. Because of him, I got a chance to meet her and her friends. They were very nice. Reagan and Toya are worried about Lacy Ann. And they are scared. When they found out that their principal wanted to suspend them, they say they were not shocked.

"He did warn us," Toya said. "But friends are more important than hair." I agree.

And how does Lacy feel to have such awesome friends?

Lacy said, "I've been friends with Toya and Reagan since kindergarten. Our dads golf together. We're in and out of each other's houses all the time. It means so much to me that they would do something like this to show their support. They are the best friends in the world."

Toya is on the honor roll and the volleyball team. She also takes dance in her spare time. Reagan is in chorus and orchestra; Lacy Ann was in chorus and orchestra, too. However, now she is being homeschooled while she gets treatment.

(continued)

Still, Toya and Reagan visit her every day.

Reagan said she and her parents hope they can change the headmaster's mind.

"When we found out about Lacy's illness, we told her we had her back no matter what. My mom and dad understand and they support me. They want to try and work this out with the school."

Toya's father is Maxim Edgar Mayhew, the attorney who advertises on WKBD. Mr. Mayhew, she said, is considering legal action if the school fails to reverse the girls' suspensions.

"This was something I had to do. Period. If it makes some people uncomfortable, they need to get over it," Toya said.

I agree with Toya. I hope they can work it out. If not, I hope Mr. Mayhew gets all up in it— and by "it" I mean the school's business.

Shaving your head to support a sick friend should not get anybody kicked out of school. And standing up for a friend is something to be honored, not punished!

I☆I☆I☆I

Everybody was talking about the article.

"What were they like in person?" they all asked. Mrs. G. said she was really proud. We even had a TV reporter show up to talk to me about why I wrote it. I kinda think Aunt Tina put them up to it after I e-mailed her a link to the school paper, but still, it was cool. Mrs. G. chimed in to say something about encouraging all her students to speak up, and I told them I just plain thought the policy was dumb and had to do something about it.

Sara hugged me. Lauren high-fived. Becks told me she was proud.

"I'd totally cut off my hair for you guys," I said. "Anytime!" When Becks picked me up and twirled me around, I didn't even put up a fight. Well, not much of one. We goofed around a little in the halls until the bell rang.

After that, the week got back to normal. In between homework and developing my new journalistic skills, I was still worried about how to raise enough money to get our sixth graders to D.C. Not to mention worrying about stuff like the speeches that all class presidents had to give AND trying to help us win the thousand-dollar scholarship for our school.

It was time to focus.

All week long, my classmates had been coming up to me telling me their ideas.

"Can we take a limo instead of a bus?" asked one boy about our transportation to D.C.

"What about sightseeing? Do you think we can rent a helicopter when we get there? I saw that once on the Discovery Channel," said another kid.

"Know what'd be cool? If we flew to D.C. in a private jet," said a girl from my Civics class.

It was as if they had no clue how money—or the world—worked. I was a businesswoman. I knew about adding and subtracting. I knew about the bottom line— that the budget is not negotiable.

Still, I was determined. I made a list of our upcoming fund-raisers:

1. Bake sale at tonight's high school football game. (I was all set with trays I'd baked and packaged at the bakery. Goal—sell 144 cupcakes at $1.50 apiece. We could make $216!)

2. Garage Cleanup on Saturdays. $20 per garage.

3. Yard Work After Church. $20 per yard.

I'd posted all the details in the *Blueberry Chronicle*, and they were approved by Principal Striker, so ha! No idea-stealing allowed, Braxton!

Mr. G. made announcements asking for volunteers, too, so everything was all worked out. We had a plan; now it was time to execute.

For the bake sale, we would work in teams so we could cover more ground. Lauren and I would work at the main concession stand, Sara and Becks would work the home-field side, and Ebony Loudermill and Britney

Dial would sell cupcakes in the stands on the visitors' side during the game.

Sounds simple, right?

Everyone showed up pretty much on time. I gave Britney and Ebony a double-decker tray holding forty-eight cupcakes; I gave an identical tray to Becks and Sara.

Once they left, Lauren and I set up in the concession stand. The women selling fried chicken wings, catfish and white bread, French fries, hamburgers, and hot dogs, along with sodas, chips, and candy bars, were nice and helpful.

"I know you!" said a coffee-colored woman with curly brown hair. "You that little gal from the bakery. Wetzel's."

"Yes, ma'am," I said.

The women said they were all for a girl learning how to make money at an early age. They even high-fived me.

Cool Michigan air and a backdrop of a million stars made it the perfect night for football. The stadium was packed. Selling all of our cupcakes should have been easy.

By the start of the third quarter, Lauren and I had

sold all of ours. We earned seventy-two dollars. Off to a good start, I thought.

Then, when the game ended, I needed to collect cash from everyone else.

So I found my way to Britney and Ebony.

"How'd you do?" I asked.

"We sold all our cupcakes, I think," Ebony said. Uh...*you think*? They're either sold or not sold. *Be easy*, I told myself.

When I asked for the money, they gave me sixty-five dollars.

"Where's the rest?"

They looked at each other. Britney said, "That's all we have."

Um, what? I said, "Well, if you sold all the cupcakes, there should be seventy-two dollars."

And she was like, "Um, I don't know. I think this one dude, his name is Martel—"

"No, Brit," Ebony cut in, "his name is Darnell."

"Are you sure?" Britney asked.

"Yeah, it's Darnell. He's friends with my brother. He got, like, six cupcakes and was supposed to come back with the money."

"I think he forgot," said Ebony. Then, squinting really hard, like thinking was making her head hurt, she looked at Brit and said, "Maybe his name *is* Martel...."

Really, girls? Really? I took a deep breath and told myself this was the kind of colorful story that would look good in a book about my life when I grew up to be famous and rich. So I didn't karate chop anybody in the neck.

"It's okay, it's okay," I said. "Thank you for your help. Hope to see you tomorrow at Oak Woods Park."

The two of them walked away, still arguing over whether the non-paying boy was named Martel or Darnell.

It didn't take long to find Sara and Becks. Sara's pinkness practically glowed.

"So, how'd you guys do?" I asked, plopping onto the bleachers next to them. I was all ready to share the crazy story of Ebony and Britney, but the goofy look on Sara's face stopped me. Becks was texting furiously, her face glowing in the phone's light.

"Brianna, it's so wonderful!" Sara said. "Becks got a date with Bakari!"

Ever have that feeling like you've stepped on a rake and got smacked in the forehead by the handle? *Dwoing!*

I felt so tired. "Becks, really. Congratulations. I'm happy for you. But I've got to get up really early tomorrow. If I can get the cupcake holder and the money from the sale, I'm gonna go. Grandpa texted. He's waiting. Anybody need a ride?"

Sara looked at me and said, "Oh, the cupcakes." She pushed the container to me.

"We didn't get to sell all of them because Becks was texting Bakari, and I was helping her figure out what to say," she said.

"We'll totally help again next week," Becks said. "Promise we'll sell more next time."

I opened the lid. Out of forty-eight cupcakes, only twelve were missing. The remaining cupcakes looked like they'd been poked and sat on.

"You only sold twelve?" I couldn't hide my disappointment.

Sara stood quickly and wrapped her arms around my shoulders.

"You're missing the important thing here, Bree. Becks is in love. It's all so romantic. We'll tell you all about it tomorrow."

"Here!" Becks shoved a wad of cash into my hand, then she and Sara raced off toward the parking lot.

In my mind, I heard Red's drawly voice saying, "Ouuuuuuuusome!"

Yeah, a whole eighteen bucks. D.C., here we come!

Sometimes, being a sixth grader was so hard.

One good thing, though. I got a text from Toya, one of the girls from the hospital.

Hey, BJustice—wanted u to know, Hdmaster let us come back to school. Did u know the *Freep* contacted him after your article was posted? Thanx from all.

Civics Journal
Ancient Rome and Middle School

Spartacus was a slave who became a mighty gladiator. The people loved him because he spoke to
them like they mattered. Because he knew what it
was like to be one of them.

Okay, I had always considered myself to
be a Spartacus, at least where my friends were
concerned. They always came to me for advice
because I understood them. I looked out for them.

This thing with the cupcakes, though...I was
not feeling it at all.

In middle school, Spartacus would have been
one of those jock boys always talking about football. He'd have hung out in the hallway, leaning up
against the columns, looking chill.

I wanted to be like that. I thought I was like that.

But listening to Becks and Sara go on about
being in love and everything, it made my stomach
hurt. I didn't understand them—and honestly, I
didn't want to.

7

Pantomime

Saturday, October 25

The weekend started out fine. By eleven thirty on Saturday morning, we had almost thirty kids ready to work. Mr. G. was there. So were my uncle Earl and a friend of his, Mr. Otis. They both had clunker pickups. We needed them to haul away trash after we cleaned garages.

We explained to everyone that Saturday was for garage cleaning only. Sunday was yard work. "I've already talked to the homeowners association people for approval. They are expecting us to charge twenty dollars per house because that's what we agreed to, okay?"

A lot of head nodding. I was standing on top of

the base of a statue so I could see everybody. Beau Brattley, Braxton's little brother, stood near the back with his hands in his pockets. Lauren was nearby; Red, too. Becks and Sara were off to the side somewhere. Apparently, Bakari was among the volunteers and love was in the air.

I worked on forgetting how mad I was at Becks and Sara. Trying to portray the mellow calm of a true leader. Today was a new day.

With the help of Mr. G., Mrs. G., and another sixth-grade teacher we'd recruited, we broke into groups and headed in different directions. We'd passed out the block numbers and streets of the neighborhoods where we expected the most participation.

Our group was led by Mrs. G. We went to three houses before we found an old lady who agreed to let us clean her garage. She said her name was Mrs. Elderberry. "But you can call me Ellie."

Ellie was small and frail-looking, but her eyes were clear and alert. When she opened her garage door, I about fainted. One side was packed from top to bottom with just about everything you could imagine. The other side looked like it had been hit by a tornado. She wanted us to clean up the tornado side.

She also had nine cats—all named Johnny.

"After my late husband," she explained.

We were introduced to Johnny Earl, Johnny Ray, Johnny Mae, and Rooster Johnny.

She said, "Rooster Johnny's got all the girl cats 'round here worked up."

Johnny Ray, a plump orange thing, took the opportunity to use a hidden litter box near the washer and dryer.

Click snapped a LEGO figure's head on and off. He made a choking sign with his hands. I giggled. He whispered, "Smells like Johnny Ray's got some digestive issues!"

We all held our breath and got to work.

I got us organized, broke up tasks, and gave everyone an assignment. It went pretty well. Hendrix, a boy from my language arts class, was hilarious, and I enjoyed working with him. Click, too. I realized I'd spent more time with Click since school began than just about anybody other than my girls.

"I have an idea for our next mini-film," he said as we held our noses while removing boxes filled with used litter.

"What? Something in a cemetery, because we'll all be dead from toxic fumes?"

He laughed. "No. I was thinking we could do something funny with a kid fund-raising for his school. You know? Have a character going door-to-door trying to sell candy. Each time someone more and more ridiculous could answer the door."

We both started cracking up. I said, "Or . . . what if the kid kept trying to sell candy to the same person? Only each time the person gets madder and madder."

"Yeah! What if we made his head explode 'cause he was so mad!"

Now we were doubling over laughing. But when this kid from the bus who always stares at me weird came over, Click changed. Acting more like a boy-boy than—I don't know—Click.

He and the dude gave each other complicated fist bumps.

"Click!" shouted the dude. "You're my man!"

Click-click.

90

Bus Dude answered the clicks with a nod. His eyes went from inky dark to a soft brown. A slow smile spread over his lips.

When I looked at Click, he wore an unexpected grin.

"Click?" I said, but he just backed away, whistling.

It was weird. I felt myself blushing.

But Bus Dude just laughed.

"When we finish here, can we go to my granny's? She's waiting for us to do her house, too," he said. She lived around the corner, and when we got to her house, she was waiting for us.

It turned out his name was Romeo James. And his grandmother was the sweetest thing. She gave him a big hug and he grinned like it was his birthday. A kid who loved his grandma that much was okay by me.

"Hey, Grandma. These are my friends," he said. She gave each of us a hug, then told us what she wanted cleaned up. When we finished, she insisted that we meet her in the backyard for lunch. It was all set up—tuna fish, turkey, and fried bologna sandwiches, along with chips and lemonade. The cold air rushed over us and kicked up some leaves. Still, for Michigan, it was fairly warm and sunny. A good day.

I☆I☆I☆I

"Why do you stare at me like that on the bus?" I finally asked Romeo between bites of tuna fish.

"Like what?" he asked.

"You know."

"You know, too."

I blushed again. Maybe I shouldn't have brought it up.

He looked down, and it seemed like maybe he was blushing a bit, too. Either that, or the cold breezes were turning his brown cheeks red.

"Don't worry, girl," he said, getting all street on me. "I'm messing with you, that's all. You know you look good, though. But when a brother's name is Romeo, well..."

Click said, "He's gotta walk the walk. If my name was Romeo, maybe I'd play with girls instead of LEGO pieces. We all gotta have our thing, right?"

My eyes went wide. *Julio Ramon Garcia!* They fist-bumped again, and I shook my head.

The two of them talked and it was clear they'd gone to elementary together. Romeo James played football for

a city league but was here because they had the week off;
Click had played football, too, but got hurt last year and
had to have surgery. His mom didn't want him to play
anymore.

"We miss you, man," Romeo was saying as we
cleaned up our lunch trash.

Listening to the two of them, I was having such a
good time that I forgot to check on the other groups.

Big mistake.

When I finally remembered to call Mr. G., it was
almost the end of our workday. He answered his phone
after one ring. He didn't sound good.

"I just sent a text to my wife," he said. "Gather your
troops and meet back at Oak Woods Park. Quickly."

Once we'd all assembled, Mr. G., usually so
enthusiastic, growled his disappointment with "certain
individuals."

He said some kids had been asked to leave one
home because they seemed more interested in goofing
around and throwing leaves at one another than doing
any real work. I noticed Becks look up quickly, then look
at the ground.

That wasn't the worst of it, however. Middle school's

poorest sport—that would be Braxton Brattley—managed to surpass even his own low-down dirty dirtiness.

Despite being in seventh grade and having no reason to be here, he'd hooked up with his brother and a few others to mess things up even more!

At one house, they asked for fifty dollars and the guy actually paid it. When another group of kids showed up and asked to clean the same man's garage, he was shocked to learn that the rate was twenty dollars. He got so angry that when Mr. G. arrived to try to straighten everything out, he had to refund the dude's cash entirely and apologize.

Brattley and his Band of Boneheads didn't stop there, though. They also offered to do yard work, even though we weren't supposed to be doing yards. So, of course, someone from the homeowners association stopped by and asked what they were doing.

Those little trolls had the nerve to get smart with the lady and told her to mind her own business. Then they BURNED THE LEAVES.

Uh, hello! Leaf burning is not cool. And IT'S AGAINST THE LAW.

The homeowners association lady was not happy. She called the police.

The police were not happy. They tracked down Mr. G.

Now Mr. G. was even more unhappy.

He was yelling at all of us, but some kids weren't listening. It reminded me of something he said in class about pantomime and how it worked in ancient Rome. How actors would do them in these open-air theaters. And how Roman audiences were notorious for talking during the show, kinda like what happens if you go see a scary movie out at Northland Mall.

He said the actors had to gesture a lot so the audience would understand.

Lauren must have been thinking the same thing. She leaned over to me, whispering, "If Mr. G. waves his hands around any wilder he's going to fly back in time."

All I could say was, *"Guuuuuuurl!"*

We tallied up our earnings and left the park in silence. Having Mr. G. look so disappointed was a big letdown.

By the end of the weekend, I smelled like grass,

dirt, and despair. Our combined total for three days' worth of fund-raising opportunities:

> $155 for cupcake sales
> $200 for garage cleaning
> $80 for yard work
> _____
> $435 total

Not terrible, but...math don't lie. We were going to have to come up with something a lot better or we'd never earn enough by our deadline.

When Katy's one-eyed cat hopped onto my bed, I didn't even bother shooing it away. And don't tell anybody, but when a few tears of frustration slid down my cheeks, the mangy little thing licked my face, and I didn't even mind. I buried my fingers in its fur and drifted to sleep wondering what I could do to make our trip a reality.

Monday, October 27

Gossip tickled the hallways and dangled in the air like moss on cemetery trees. (That's both a metaphor and a simile. When you spend four hours on a sofa with your dad watching horror flicks over the weekend, you get these kinds of thoughts.)

A lot of the gossip had to do with me and how it didn't look like I could raise enough money for our trip.

My life had gone from everybody telling me I was awesome on Friday (after all the attention about the newspaper article), to being the latest victim of the Mumble Mafia—kids who talk about you right in front of your face, only they mumble it. The Mumble Mafia are the worst kind of bullies. *I didn't have time for that.*

So when two girls and two boys in sixth grade started that nonsense, I shut it down.

They were, like, "Mmm-hmm, she need to go somewhere and get some better ideas before nobody makes it to D.C."

I was standing right there. RIGHT. THERE. But they couldn't be bothered to just turn and look at me. No, they had to start mumbling to one another. Let me tell you, middle schoolers and future middle schoolers. You let kids like that bring you down and you don't even have a name anymore.

So I was, like, "Um, first of all, none of you are even on the list to go to D.C., so what're you even talking about?"

And one of the girls was, like, "Um, excuse *you*, but nobody was talking to you."

I got right in her face. Not yelling. Not cursing. Just standing my ground.

I said, "All of y'all need to be way more worried about your own business rather than trying to talk about me or anybody else. Oh, and by the way, you really need to do something positive with that breath!"

Then I walked away. When you drop a bomb on the Mumble Mafia, just walk away.

Despite that negativity, I still had sixth graders coming up to me with elaborate schemes to make money—ideas that had no chance of working.

One boy suggested a hip-hop car wash. He said we could ask famous rappers to come down and help us raise money. He said he saw it once on his favorite TV show. I told him I'd get right on that.

A girl told me she thought it would be great if we held a dog wash. Like a car wash, but for dogs. Not a completely lame idea, I thought. Until she informed me that she wouldn't volunteer because she didn't like washing dogs, but she would bring her dog if we did it.

At least one good thing happened. Becks and Sara both sent texts first thing Monday morning.

From Becks:

```
I <3 YOU BREE-BREE
```

And Sara's text was a photo of the four of us from third grade. Back then, Sara wore her hair in pigtails. Her eyes were a little red. This one kid in class, Todd Hampton, I called Toady Todd because when he was pushing kids around, his voice croaked like a frog's. Anyway, he was teasing her, calling her "black Japanese." Because her mother is African American and her father, Korean. Anyway, when kids made fun of her, slanting their eyes, she'd cry. And that day, boy was she crying. But Becks and I told her she was beautiful. We squeezed our cheeks together and made goofy faces at the camera. We were sisters.

In the photo, all four of us stood with our cheeks pressed together. United. Like we were one person.

Sara's text read:

ALWAYS SISTERS, ALWAYS LOVE

I thought about the three friends at the hospital. Their photo in the paper, how they shared a look of complete oneness. It reminded me of this photo of the four of us. Only...looking at the old photo on my phone's screen, I realized how different we all were now. It was like looking at four girls I used to know. Weird, right?

At least we weren't fighting anymore. We even made plans to go to the movies on Saturday. And when I was moping about the trip, Becks said, "Don't get all worried like you always do, Brianna. We're going to make it. I just know it. I can't wait 'til we get to D.C. It's gonna be sick!"

Her enthusiasm made me feel better—and worse. Better because it showed she still cared about the trip. But what if the trip didn't happen at all?

Civics Journal
Ancient Rome and Middle School

Pantomime in ancient Rome started as a form of theater.

It was popular for the Romans to put on plays, but the audience was usually so loud that the actors couldn't be heard. So they had to learn to tell the story with big gestures and colorful set pieces.

Now, that is definitely like middle school. Only, in our version of pantomime, it's like all of us middle schoolers are the actors AND the audience. It's like we're constantly trying to put on a show so others will know what we think or how we feel.

Our lives are one big show.

And most of the time, we're not sure if anyone is listening.

8

Furies

Tuesday, October 28

Baking helped to chill me out, but it didn't solve my problems. Becks and Sara, even though they apologized, were still acting weird. And when I asked them if they wanted to help with my first catering job, they were, like, "We'll see."

Hmph!

Although I was tired of everybody acting like money was the only thing that mattered to me, I did need to focus on how to make enough money for our trip. And if I didn't come up with a killer speech for the conference, our school might not win the thousand-dollar prize, either.

In Civics, Mr. G. once again ran down what was expected of us at the conference.

He said, "Young people! Young people! May I have your attention, please!" Whenever he called us "young people" in that high-pitched tone, we knew he wasn't playing around.

He went on and told us how we were expected to conduct ourselves. How we would have the opportunity of a lifetime.

"You will be given access to the inner workings of the American government. You will participate in workshops, take day trips, and have the opportunity to show your knowledge during a lively competition on comparing our governmental structure with that of the ancient Romans," he said.

Then he turned to me, his eyes shining like he was crossing the finish line while carrying the Olympic torch.

He said, "Brianna, I don't want to put too much pressure on you. Amanda finished second in the speech category, but that doesn't mean you have to do the same thing. I believe in you. Just do your best!"

Sooooo, no pressure there, right?

Truth was, I really wanted to win. Braxton Brattley had definitely *not* won when he was sixth-grade president. If I brought home first place, it would shut him up for good!

Still, none of that mattered if we couldn't even pay for the trip. I turned my attention back to raising more money.

Grandpa offered to drive me out to businesses that agreed to donate their bottles and cans so I could recycle them for cash. In Michigan, that's ten cents per can or bottle. Not exactly gold bars, but if you do it enough, it starts to add up.

When I wasn't doing homework or thinking up speech topics, I was raking leaves, even cleaning our garage. I also wrote letters to supermarket chains and other local businesses trying to see if we could get sponsors. The letter-writing had been Mr. G.'s idea.

"Baby, you're looking a little tired," Mom said one night. She was standing in my bedroom doorway; I was seated on my bed, legs crisscrossed, going over a list on my clipboard.

"Lots to do, Ma!" I said, without looking up.

"I spoke with your uncle Al in D.C. He's looking forward to seeing us when we go down there next month," she said. Mom was one of the chaperones for our trip. I glanced up.

"Me, too, Mom. But, please, no offense, I need to work. I have so much to do!"

She said, "Well, it'll have to wait. It's bedtime."

I said, "But..."

She didn't even try to listen. Just turned off my light switch. It made me so mad, I hopped up, flipped it right back on. Kept on working. She just didn't understand how much pressure I was under.

I wedged my earbuds in my ears. I was singing along with an old Mariah Carey song. Well, trying to sing along, as I read over the next steps of my plan:

☆ Recruit a few more kids to register for trip—more kids paying means more money coming in.

☆ Reread back issues of *Executive, Jr.* magazine. (In case I am chosen for an interview, I want to know how to play it!)

☆ Figure out our "purpose." (As president of the sixth grade, I feel we're pretty weak in the "purpose" area. I'm not even sure I know what it means, really, but explaining our purpose is the whole theme of the speeches.)

I never even heard Mom come back into the room.

She looked at me, that one eyebrow—I call it the Executioner—cocked and loaded. She gave me such a nasty stink eye I needed a tetanus shot.

I took out the earbuds. Turned off the iPod. Slid my books and clipboard to the floor and slipped under the cover. She flipped off the lights—again.

"Don't make me come back in here, little girl."

Hmph!

I was not a little girl. I was a businesswoman. A leader.

So why did I secretly wish she would rush back in and tell me exactly how to fix the sixth grade?

Wednesday, October 29

A happy surprise was waiting when I walked into journalism class.

Mrs. G. called me to her desk.

She said, "Brianna, I'd like you to consider joining the newspaper club."

The newspaper club was mostly seventh and eighth graders. Sixth graders joined by invitation only.

I said, "Really?"

"Really!" she replied.

BAM!

After school, I texted home and told Grandpa I wouldn't be on the bus. Told him I was staying after school for a club meeting.

Me:

I can walk to the bakery from here.

Grandpa:

Call me when you leave the school. Don't text, Brianna. Call. Then call me when you get to the bakery.

Me:

Okay.

The only other sixth grader I saw when I entered Mrs. G.'s classroom was Red.

She gave a little wave. I waved back. Eventually, we wound up sitting together. I think maybe we were both a little intimidated. And we both would rather die than admit it.

"Um, you know you're the star of the rumor mill," I said.

She gave a fake shiver and wiggled her fingers together.

"Oh, yay!" she sang out. "So glad to keep y'all entertained."

"The one about your daddy being a rancher and your mother being a former Miss Texas—that's one of my favorites," I said.

She shrugged. "That one's almost true. My favorite is the one about me faking this accent to get attention. I mean, don't get me wrong. I love the way folks talk back home, but it's not like I'm running around looking for ways to draw attention to myself."

I laughed. "Uh, no offense, dude, but you've gotta be kidding me. You're dressed in head-to-toe black and your hair is Kool-Aid red. *Guuuuurl*, you are not incognito."

She flashed a wicked grin, when Amanda, the girl in charge of the newspaper, said it was time to get started.

Amanda Keene was an eighth grader. When she was in sixth, she was class president, too. Her D.C. speech was amazing, and placed second out of a hundred and eleven at the conference, according to Mr. G. She was smart, well liked, and dedicated. The kind of girl I wanted to be when I got to eighth grade.

She seemed really motivated, too. A dry, heavy lump rose in my throat. I felt my skin prickle and a thin line of sweat bubble up on my forehead.

If I said the wrong thing in here, I could look like an idiot in front of a room full of seventh and eighth graders. SEVENTH and EIGHTH graders. And a former presidential goddess.

It'd be certain doom to look like a loser in front of her.

So I chewed on my lower lip and stayed quiet, as an assistant editor, a boy named Mark Canny, started talking about Detroit.

He said, "How many people here think they're not from Detroit?" Several hands went up. I played it safe, keeping my hand low. Red didn't say anything. We lived outside Detroit. About twenty minutes south, near Southfield, in Orchard Park.

Mark looked at the hands, nodded. Looked at Amanda.

She said, "Now, when the Detroit Lions made it to the NFL playoffs, how many people were cheering or trying to 'represent' for Detroit?"

Hmm... now even other seventh and eighth graders seemed to hesitate. Hands up? Hands down? No one seemed certain. Still, several hands shot up.

Again, Mark nodded. He looked at us for a long time.

He said, "We hear stories every day about how the city of Detroit went broke. What do you guys think of that?"

We talked about the city. How easy it was for kids like us, kids from the suburbs, to act all superior. Like people in Detroit were second-class citizens. I hated when kids acted that way. I loved Detroit! Had loved it since I was a kid. Going downtown in the summer to Hart Plaza for the festivals. Going to my favorite Greek restaurant for gyros. That spicy lamb meat grilled piping hot, placed on a soft pita, and topped with this tasty, creamy Greek dressing and onions. Just thinking about it was making me hungry.

One kid, a boy in eighth, said, "Nobody better say nothing bad about the city. We're all Detroit. One hundred percent!"

Several kids clapped, including me. Thank you, eighth-grade dude.

Then Amanda said, "Brianna, I've heard you're a little businesswoman, selling cupcakes at Wetzel's. So what do you think about the new trend among Detroit businesses?"

My brain started to shut down. I was in total panic mode. Huh? What was she talking about? I was doomed! Was my mouth hanging open? Had the word *loser* tattooed itself onto my forehead?

As I bit on my lip, little flicks of information clicked in my mind. Gradually, the information bits turned into a story. Articles I'd read. *Deep breath.*

Please don't sound stupid . . . Please don't sound stupid . . . Please don't sound stupid . . .

"You mean like the start-up businesses or the new

businesses that move into abandoned houses and use them to test business ideas? Like that?"

Amanda and Mark nodded. So did several others. I could feel Red's bright blue-eyed gaze on the side of my face. Another deep breath. I kept going.

I said, "I think it's...awesome. If I were older, I might try something like that, too."

Knots of fear twisted in my belly. A pressure inside me swelled. I couldn't let these older, smarter kids think I was lame!

Amanda said, "See, Mark! I told you she was smart!"

It was like all the pressure in my body set off an explosion of joy inside of me. I was so relieved, I felt dizzy.

Since my aunt Tina was a business writer, I'd heard her and my dad talk about how so much of Detroit was in disrepair. Houses were left empty because people couldn't afford to live in them. Crime was up because people didn't have jobs and because poor leadership left the city too broke to pay for stuff like police officers or even streetlights.

It was a bad situation.

But Aunt Tina had told me about small businesses, like restaurants and clothes designers, who set up shop in these abandoned homes. They'd clean them up and get power and water running for thirty days or so and do their thing. Send out tweets and use other social media to let people know what they had.

I thought it sounded really cool and fantasized about what it'd be like to take over an abandoned house, clean it up, and fill it with cupcakes!

Amanda once again cut into my brain drift. "Your story about the girl with cancer was really cool," she said. "Showed a lot of initiative. I want you to think about writing a positive story about Detroit. Even though our school is outside the city, what happens in Detroit affects all of us. Just like what happens to those girls you wrote about affects all of us in some way. So think about a story idea. We can talk about it later."

When the meeting was over, my head was spinning.

Which was why, half an hour after I got to the bakery, I was surprised when Mrs. Wetzel told me I had a call. I thought it might be someone wanting to talk about another catering job.

Instead, it was Grandpa. A very unhappy Grandpa.

"Brianna Diane Justice..."

Uh-oh. This couldn't be good. Diane had been the

name of my grandmother—his wife. He did not use it lightly.

"I thought I told you to call me when you left school..."

Aw, dang!

I said, "Oh, but I—"

He cut me off. Didn't even listen. He said, "Oh, but nothing! I told you to call me when you left the school, Brianna. I told you to call me when you got to the bakery. What if something had happened? What if you were in trouble of some kind?"

No matter what I said, I was wrong. After a few seconds, I stopped trying to say anything. When he finished yelling at me, I went back to my workstation. Took my phone out. I had been trying to explain that my phone was dead. Soon as I plugged it in and sat it on the counter, it beeped. I had three texts—one from Daddy, two from Mom. All were yelling at me.

You'd think that'd be enough stink to throw on a girl for one day. Sadly, you'd be wrong. A few minutes before it was time to go home, in walked the Brattley Brats!

Like always, Beau hung back. Braxton came over

to the cupcakes. He leaned over the display case, peering into the glass. He whispered, "I'd like to order a vanilla cupcake with a side order of sixth-grade presidential failure." His voice was low and sweet, like he was talking to a snake at a tea party.

So, staring through the other side of the case, I made my voice all singsong-y and bright. "Sorry, but we're all out of that flavor. However, I did just bake a batch of get-over-yourself muffins. Maybe you'd like a dozen?"

He stood. I stood. He glared hard. I glared harder. Stalemate.

I couldn't help noticing then that Beau didn't do... anything. Just stood there, looking back and forth between me and his brother. And this was the dude Braxton wanted to take over the sixth grade?

Braxton made his usual stink-face of disapproval.

He said, "You're the one who needs to get over yourself. Have you even picked a topic for your speech yet?"

That stung. I hadn't. I tried not to let it show. But it did.

"I knew it!"

"Don't worry about my speech," I said, weakly.

He turned and headed for the door. They bought

no cupcakes. Braxton said over his shoulder, "When you fail, Mr. G. is going to be so disappointed! I might *not* even say I told you so."

Thursday, October 30

While most everyone was talking about a zombie apocalypse and how to survive, or just planning what they were doing for Halloween, I was feeling even more pressure.

From my family getting all pissy because I'd forgotten to call Grandpa, to having my classmates whisper about whether I was a lousy leader, to a few of my best friends acting like idiots—it was all getting to me.

In my Home Ec class, things sort of just bubbled over and went *SPLAT.*

Everybody knew how I felt about our teacher, Mrs. Bwöring. She pronounced it "baring." Said the *w* was silent. I wished *she* would be silent. It was supposed to be a cooking class, but all she did was talk about budgets and meal planning. She sucked all the life out of a class I'd hoped would be my favorite.

When I got to class, my head ached and so did my

shoulders. My hands and arms, too. My whole body just felt tired. I couldn't stop thinking about all we had to do to get ready for the D.C. trip. And as soon as I walked into class, Mrs. Bwöring was on me.

"No gum chewing in class, Miss Justice." But I wasn't. Chewing. Gum!

Then:

"Stop dragging your feet, Miss Justice."

And then:

"This isn't a bake sale, Miss Justice. I am trying to equip young minds with tools for the rest of their lives."

What can I say? I just sort of snapped.

I slouched in my seat, crossed my arms over my chest. I said, "Do you even know how to cook?"

Several heads turned in my direction. Mrs. Bwöring stopped in the aisle, her back to me. She turned slowly, looking at me.

She took a step closer. Acid burned in my stomach. I was so wrong. I knew it. This was not leadership behavior. But something was pushing at me from the inside. It was like I couldn't take one more thing.

Mrs. Bwöring was tall. Like NBA tall. She had dark skin and dark hair that she tied in a bun. She always wore dresses and flats. Now she stood towering over my desk, her shadow long and ominous.

For some reason, her standing over me just made me madder.

I looked at her, and it was on.

"This is the worst class I've ever taken!"

"MISS JUSTICE! You will show me proper respect or I will send you to see the principal." I jumped to my feet. It was like I'd been completely possessed by some back-talking spirit.

Glaring up at her, I said: "Please! Oh, please! Send me to Principal Striker's office. At least there I won't have to look at your ugly flowered dresses or smell the moldy mothballs!"

By now, several kids were laughing and hooting. I got my wish. Kicked out of class. At first, I was glad. GLAD! My newfound bad-girl moment had my veins on fire with rebellious joy.

Then I got to the stairway and realized I could get expelled—or worse, removed as class president. I nearly passed out. I was slumped against the wall outside the girls' bathroom when I felt my phone vibrate in my book bag. Using your phone during school is an offense punishable by death or something, but I figured I was already in trouble. What did it even matter? I reached over, fished it out of my bag, and saw I had a text.

From Lauren? How could she already know what happened?

Then I read it and my heart stopped. The message had nothing to do with me. It read:

> Did u hear? Becks is leaving honors program.

I felt as if a switch had flipped. Becks was going to leave me all alone in Lame Land?

Tears stung my eyes. My heart beat an angry rhythm in my chest. Back in fifth grade, I never would have fought with a teacher. And Becks never would have quit something that she was good at. But I was learning more and more that fifth grade was a long time ago.

The Land of Fake-Believe was no fairy tale. I needed to get far, far away!

Civics Journal
Ancient Rome and Middle School

Back in ancient Rome they loved their gods and goddesses. There was a group of goddesses called Furies. You know, as in fur-i-ous?

Anyway, right now, I feel like I'm down with the Furies. Feel like my insides are getting squeezed to death. The ancient Furies were all about revenge. Maybe that was the same for me. I was angry, not just at my Home Ec teacher, but at my parents, all my other teachers, the other students, and myself.

Today, I am a Fury.

For real!

9

Hail Caesar? Hail No!

Have you ever done something even though you knew in your bones how wrong it was?

I made a spur-of-the-moment decision. Something I almost never did. I was a planner. A girl with a clipboard. In the back of my mind, I knew how angry my parents would be and how upset the school would be if I got caught. Not to mention how dangerous it was.

But I needed to do something that was totally *not* me. And it felt like it wasn't even *me* doing it!

So I did it. Took off from school and caught a city bus out of the 'burbs and into downtown Detroit.

My heart pumped hard and fast. An hour and ten minutes later, when we got to Grand River Avenue, I climbed off the bus and hopped on this train called the people mover that went all over downtown.

Am I nuts?

I can't be here!

It was like the good part of me was fighting with the lost and confused and ANGRY me. In fact, I hadn't really thought about how frustrated, confused, and angry I was until I started climbing off that bus.

When my phone vibrated, I sucked in some air. Grandpa. I sent back a text.

I'm here.

Here was supposed to be the library. Lying made my head hurt. I slumped low in the hard plastic seat of the elevated train. It grunted along the tracks, stopping just long enough to let passengers on and off. My mind kept replaying the last several days.

My failure at raising enough money for our trip, no matter what I did.

Having Mrs. BORing get all up in my face.

Becks leaving the honors program. Why?

The questions pinged around my brain. A tightness squeezed from my chest to my stomach. Outside, the sky stretched over us, gray and sad, like a pale face in despair.

It was time to make a decision. Too late to turn back now, to avoid getting in trouble. Might as well make the most of it. At least, that was what I hoped.

So I started to pay attention to what I was passing, looking for all the things I loved about Detroit. Like the Atheneum Suite Hotel. Mom, Katy, and I stayed there once for a girls' weekend. We had massages and got mani-pedis. It was awesome.

I realized we must be in Greektown. I got off at the stop and raced down the steps. Lunch at school had consisted of gray lumpy stuff poured over brown lumpy stuff. I'd eaten an apple. Now my stomach didn't just growl—it roared.

The New Parthenon Restaurant served the most amazing gyros. It didn't take long to get served. I must have been hungrier than I thought, because it was like that gyro had never even existed, I'd eaten so fast. When I felt full, I looked around the room.

Ancient Rome stole a lot of ideas about everything from the Greeks. So it wasn't any wonder that the decor of the restaurant, which was supposed to look Greek, also resembled a lot of the pictures we'd seen of ancient Rome.

It was weird, you know? All school year, Mr. G. had been telling us this stuff, trying to get us ready for the D.C. trip and the competition. Learning the vocabulary words, looking at photos of old buildings, we just thought of it as homework.

But here I was in Greektown, seeing how the influence of ancient Rome and Greece affected modern times.

"You sure finished that up!" said the waiter. His eyebrows were fat and bushy. He had a mustache like Luigi in *Mario Kart*. I felt stuffed—it was the best gyro ever.

I calculated his tip, deciding to leave 20 percent. Sometimes when people ate inside Wetzel's and I brought them their cupcakes, they'd give me a tip. Tips were awesome!

I asked if I could snap some photos of the decor with my phone. Before I left, it was starting to get darker, and I didn't have a clue what to do next. Running away to downtown Detroit had not been on the "To Do" list on my clipboard. But remembering the cool photos I took inside, I decided not to waste my journey into the big city.

I thought about the newspaper assignment Amanda had given me. Maybe instead of a regular story, I'd do a story in pictures. Show the sights and places that had meaning to me. I could even highlight the ones with the architecture or design elements we talked about in Mr. G.'s class.

Using my phone's camera, I started walking and taking photos of any buildings or architecture that stood out. The Second Baptist Church of Detroit was a historic landmark. Although the architecture had nothing to do with what we were studying, I took a picture of myself in front of it anyway. Grandpa told me how this church was part of the Underground Railroad, back when Harriet Tubman was helping slaves escape from the South. Whenever I saw the old church, it made me feel proud. When Grandma was alive, we'd come to services here sometimes.

I kept walking, lost in thought. Thinking about the speech I was supposed to write—a speech about having purpose and leadership. Thinking about people who'd been enslaved and fought for freedom. Thinking about the people who fought to get them freedom.

I did so much thinking, I lost track of time—and where I was. When I started paying attention again, I saw that the tall buildings were blocking the sky, and darkness was creeping around me. I started to get self-conscious, feeling like my brightly colored pants and hoodie—fluorescent blue and neon pink—glowed.

I watched as women in business suits rushed from building to building up and down the sidewalk. Some wore slick pantsuits with low-heeled boots, or skirts and blazers under stylish wool coats. Even young women who looked like they might have just gotten out of college wore crisp white shirts tucked into neat black jeans with boots and leather jackets.

Looking down at myself again, I realized how young I looked. I'd never thought about it that much, but maybe how you looked did affect what people thought of you. Maybe part of moving away from being just a baker to being a leader meant wearing clothes that didn't provide their own light source.

Movement and color caught my attention, coming

from a large picture window. When I drew closer, I saw that it was a dance school. Girls of all different sizes wore tights and leotards. They were stretching. Looked like they were on some sort of break.

Then I got that strange feeling you get when someone is staring at you, a prickling along my scalp. A set of bright blue eyes was on me.

It was Red!

She gave me her usual half smile and nodded toward the door. I walked down, waited. In a few minutes she stepped outside.

She wore a black hoodie over her black leotard. Pink tights went straight down into black high-tops. She'd pulled on a pair of loose-fitting white sweats that stopped just below her knees.

I didn't know what to say. "Um…"

She jumped in. "Yeah, um, so you caught me. This is my secret identity. By day I'm a regular middle school student. By night, I'm a crime-fighting ballerina in the city."

She shrugged.

I shrugged.

"How long have you been, um, saving the world?" I asked.

She said, "I started when I was three. Since I just turned twelve—"

"Nine years!"

"Wow, Justice! You're so quick with math. No wonder you're our leader."

We both laughed. Then she asked, "What're you doing down here? Are your folks around?" She looked both ways trying to spot my parents.

"Aw, you know, just sort of hanging out, I guess," I said.

Her gaze grew more intense. One eyebrow lifted.

I felt guilty. "What?"

She took a step back, the half smile back in place. "Nothing! Nothing! Just surprised to see you, that's all."

"Hey, I'm surprised to see you, too! Blueberry Hills' best-known goth girl wears a tutu. Gotta think about that one," I said, laughing.

She smiled, then her face grew serious. "Would you mind if we kept this between us?"

"Sure," I said. "But, I mean, if you've been doing this for nine years, I'll bet you're awesome. Why hide it?"

She said ballet was something in life that was just hers. She didn't have to be great and she didn't do it for recognition. "I do it because when I dance, it's like I can hear my soul. Feeling my muscles stretch beyond reason makes me feel more alive than anything in the world. I...It's personal."

"I won't say anything to anyone. Promise."

Her break was over. She rushed back inside. The glow of pink light rushed from the window and spilled over me on the darkening sidewalk. The instructor had the girls line up in rows, their backs to the window. Red's dark-cherry hair was piled into a knot on top of her head.

It didn't take long to see that Red was a magnificent dancer. Her ankles appeared incredibly thin, yet they were strong enough to hold her as she spun in tight circles or leaped through the air. Watching her made me feel like I could hear Red's soul speaking, too. All of the dancers moved as though their bodies were weightless.

Whatever was going on with me, this rebellious funk or whatever, it was time to let it go. I needed to let myself fly. And I knew I didn't have to run away to feel free.

Wish I'd thought of that sooner. 'Cause when I turned around, another set of eyes was staring at me. And they were not bright and blue.

They were angry and brown.

How had I forgotten Cadillac Place was just across the plaza? See, the old General Motors Building had been turned into government offices. Among them, a branch of the FBI.

My mom worked there. Only, she wasn't at work anymore.

She was standing on the sidewalk, staring right at me!

Friday, November 7

Jail can teach you a lot. And that's *for reals*!

Mom went ballistic when she found me in front of the dance studio downtown. She practically hyperventilated, she was yelling so much. I was put on punishment "until further notice," which I figured meant until I was old enough to drive.

The worst part had been the Big Question:

Why?

And . . . *What were you thinking, Brianna? What would make you do something so reckless?*

Mom, Daddy, Grandpa—even Katy. They all

asked me separately. And I didn't know what to say! It should have been so easy to have one of those made-for-TV moments. Me breaking into tears and confessing, "Gee whiz, Mummy and Papa, I feel so gosh-darn overwhelmed. And I'm having trouble with my friends because they'd rather act like middle school idiots than the smart young women we were back in fifth grade!"

What was I supposed to do? I couldn't admit any of that. Not without looking like a total loser.

Daddy looked so hurt and disappointed, I did have to tell him something that wasn't a complete lie. So I told him how concerned I'd been about my speech and how worried I was about trying to raise enough money for our trip. He kind of bought it, I think, because he wanted to.

Mom, on the other hand, would have put me right in prison if one would've taken me. And I was in trouble at school, too.

Anyway, after several days of no TV, no music, no baking for fun, Daddy said if I wanted to go do some work for fund-raising, I could.

Grandpa barely said two words to me, though, as we drove around collecting cans. That was tough. I loved

Grandpa so much. I'd never thought about how crappy it'd feel to disappoint him. My whole body was starting to ache, no doubt from guilt. I'd done something really stupid and now my whole family was looking at me like I was brain damaged.

School was just as bad. I was virtually Mrs. Bwöring's servant. I had to apologize in front of the whole class and move my desk up front. Next to hers. Like I was planning a jailbreak and this was her version of maximum security. Still, I felt way guilty about mouthing off to her the way I did. It was just like going off on that kid on the bus—only ten times worse.

And after my mother informed Principal Striker about me leaving school without permission, he decided that it, plus talking back in Mrs. Bwöring's class, should get me a five-day in-school suspension. That meant during lunch I had to sit onstage with other school law-breakers.

Yep! Onstage in the cafeteria. No eating with your friends. You just sit there in a chair with your lunch while everybody walks past looking at you. It was like being in a horror movie and a jail movie, combined.

Sharing the stage of shame with me were several kids I knew, including a dude in the seventh grade who thought it would be hilarious to buy one of those electronic cigarettes and bring it to school. Then record himself puff-puffing away in the boys' bathroom. Another kid, another sixth grader, was on lockdown for skipping school. Unlike me, though, she didn't get busted by her mother. Oh, no! Like the smoker, she got busted because she was posting photos of herself online. When she was supposed to be in class. How did I end up in this group? I felt so stupid.

Just as I was feeling even more sorry for myself, I heard "*Pssst! Pssst!*" and looked down. Lauren was at the foot of the stage. If one of the cafeteria monitors caught her, she'd be toast.

My eyebrows knotted. I whispered, "What?"

"Paul Geidel!" she whispered back.

Paul who? I shrugged, unable to hide my smile. Lauren was so . . . *Lauren.*

She said, "Paul Geidel holds the record for the longest time served in prison—sixty-eight years, two hundred forty-five days. Maybe I could put a nail file in your cupcake and you could pick a lock to freedom."

Her shoulders bounced up and down as she laughed at her own cleverness. Oh, that Lauren.

She looked around and spotted Mr. Ortiz holding one boy practically by the collar. Lauren glanced up at me on the stage. She whispered, "You heard from Sara or Becks today?"

I could tell she had something else to say. If you knew Lauren, you could always tell when something was up.

Lately, Sara and Becks had been almost invisible. I didn't see them in the halls and they didn't even answer my texts much anymore. Not that I'd had a chance to text all that often. All I'd been allowed to do was go home, to school, and to work at the bakery. Because I had to skip newspaper club, Amanda Keene had been forced to give my assignment to someone else. I'd texted with Sara a few times, but Becks had not texted back. And at school she was becoming more and more distant.

"What's up with them?" I half whispered down to Lauren.

Before she could answer, Mr. Ortiz placed his hand on her shoulder.

"Going back to my table, Coach!" Lauren said, without looking at him. He glared at me, then turned his back. Lauren looked back, then mouthed, "I'll text you."

Mr. Ortiz got a call on his radio. It crackled loudly. The voice was Principal Striker's.

"Could you send Brianna Justice to my office?" he said.

Even though I wasn't wearing handcuffs or shackles, I felt restricted as I trudged down to Principal Striker's office. I also felt hot and cold at the same time. Principal Striker made me wait five minutes, sitting right in front of him, while he shuffled some papers around and ignored me.

A phone buzzed on his desk. He answered, listened for a second, then said, "Bring them in."

He stared at me over the top of his glasses. His eyes were dark and stern. When the door swung open, his voice boomed, "Come in."

I couldn't believe my eyes. It was Braxton and Beau.

Braxton looked just as surprised to see me as I was to see him. After a second, he spoke first. "Principal Striker, thank you for seeing me and my brother," he said, glancing over at me, scowling.

He said, "I just want to do what's right for the school, Principal Striker." Then he went on to make this speech about why Beau should be appointed president of the whole sixth grade because I was a bad role model.

It almost made me laugh, until I saw the look on Principal Striker's face. A cold line of sweat popped onto my forehead. I felt myself start to shake on the inside.

What was happening?

I'd worked so hard.

My heart raced and I crossed my ankles to keep my knees from knocking. Did Beau Brattley want to be class president so badly that he'd gone to his brother to cook up this . . . this foolishness? I was about to say something, but Principal Striker cut me off.

He said, "There's no question that Miss Justice has exhibited behavior unbecoming of a class official."

I wanted to protest. But my throat was so dry. My face felt hot, but my skin felt cold.

What Principal Striker said next left me feeling like I'd been punched in the stomach.

He looked right at me. "Brianna, maybe you shouldn't be president of the sixth grade. . . ."

I felt myself getting light-headed. My heart raced.

Then everything went dark.

Civics Journal
Ancient Rome and Middle School

Julius Caesar was a total bada#%— Uh, I mean, tough dude.

See, he was a general in the Roman military and he led many great battles. But he was famous because he listened to the problems of Roman people and promised them a better life.

But wouldn't you know it? A bunch of stuck-up senators, afraid they'd lose their power if Caesar kept getting stronger, started plotting against him.

Well, you can guess what happened:

Like I said before, on the Ides of March, 44 BC, Caesar was assassinated. And the republic died, too. Which meant that Rome became an empire, led by a few, rather than a republic led by the many.

10

The Baths

Sunday, November 9

A furry lion pawed at me with its huge claws.

Principal Striker? Is that you?

Wait! The lion was trying to tell me something.
Had to write it down. Oh, yeah. Lion wants to go to the
museum. *What long whiskers you have, Principal Striker.
And what a fluffy tail, too. Never noticed that before.* My eyes
burned. So did my throat.

*Sooooo tired. Still... have an idea. A really, really good
idea.*

*Nice lion. Nice lion. You're very wise. Now, please, Prin-
cipal Striker, don't eat my face.*

I☆I☆I☆I

Trembling fingers. Mine. A keyboard. A message. A lion's paw? I definitely was not in the principal's office anymore.

I☆I☆I☆I

Voices floated around the room.

"...exhaustion..."

"...high fever..."

"...worn out..."

Phrases broke apart like bits of paper, ripped up and tossed like confetti. My language arts teacher would be very proud of how poetic my mind was while in the throes of fever. I felt too tired to move.

In my mind, I was waving frantically for them to come closer. Wanted to share my idea. But my eyes felt glued shut. Maybe a nap instead...

I☆I☆I☆I

By Thursday the fever was gone. I was still tired, but the worst of it had passed.

Dad said he'd received a call telling him I fainted at school. He took me to the hospital and they pumped me full of meds and sent me home. He was told my temperature was 107 degrees.

"Any higher and you might've had brain damage!" he said.

Katy said, "Daddy, are you sure you got to her in time? In fact, are you sure she didn't already have some sort of fever before?"

I made a face at her, but she smiled and squeezed my hand. Her scruffy cat was sitting on the bed, a wreath of yellowish fur around its face making it look like a tiny lion. A lion? A memory tried to struggle up from the fuzziness of my brain. But I couldn't quite make it out.

Katy said, "I know how much you hate the animals. Don't worry, I'll get her out of here. But while you were knocked out, we couldn't get her to leave your room."

My hands shot out and scooped up the cat before she had the chance to remove it.

"No!" I said, holding the cat close to me. My voice was hoarse and thick. "I want to keep her!"

The room went silent. Dad came and put his hand on my forehead. Mom squinted, looking worried. She said, "Brianna, are you sure you're all right?"

I let out a long, shaky breath. "Fine, Mom. It's just...I've kinda gotten used to the ratty old thing. I want to keep her. I'm going to name her Angel."

They all looked at me for a long moment. Then Mom nodded. "That's fine, baby. We'll talk about it later."

She started telling me about Mr. G.'s visits to the house.

"He's been here a few times. He's really worried about you. Your friends have been here, too!"

Dad rolled his eyes. "Sara, she showed up with some fuzzy concoction on her head, bright red lips. With those skinny legs, she looked like a chicken," he said.

Mom swatted him on the shoulder.

They stared at me. Mom said, "I think you need more rest. You and...um, Angel, should just be calm. I'll bring you up some juice and crackers."

I tried to object, but found myself drifting off to sleep again before they were even out of the room. By Friday, I felt much better, but Mom and Dad still wouldn't let me have any company. They wouldn't even let me use the computer.

"We should've been keeping a closer eye on you," Mom said. She had her stern-mama face on. "You've been running yourself into the ground. No wonder you've been acting like you've lost your mind lately. You've driven yourself crazy with exhaustion.

"No computer, phone, nothing before tomorrow. If your temperature continues to be good, we'll let a few folks stop in to visit," she said.

Even after I told her, "I love you, Mommy!" she wouldn't cave. She just kept telling me to take a hot bath. Said the heat would sweat out the last of the fever. I felt like a pickle.

Saturday was the Michigan vs. Michigan State game. My folks were letting a few of my friends stop by.

That was when I finally got information about what was going on.

First of all, Mr. Galafinkis had, indeed, been to the house. He told my parents that he was very proud of the work I was doing. Huh?

Then he sent an e-mail that blew my mind:

Your fund-raising ideas are excellent.
Thanks to a lot of good students and your
friends reaching out, we have accomplished
a lot. I am so sorry if the stress of making
our trip possible contributed to your ill
health. However, rest assured, we are working
hard on your behalf. The event should be
spectacular. Reaching out to the Detroit
Institute of Arts and getting their approval
like that, Brianna, was pure genius. The entire
sixth grade owes you a debt of gratitude. Get
well soon!

Sincerely,
Mr. G.

P.S. Thanks to an anonymous e-mail that
Principal Striker received about some
underhanded work on the part of Braxton
Brattley, rest assured that neither he nor his
brother will trouble you again.

I reread the e-mail several times.

What idea?

And the Detroit Institute of Arts? What was that all about? Again, a memory stuffed deep in my head struggled to free itself. Something to do with an idea that came to me when I was sick. Only I couldn't quite remember what it was.

Dad told me that he'd spoken with Principal Striker, too. Principal Striker told Dad about Braxton's attempts to overthrow the sixth-grade government. The principal wasn't going to make me step down. In fact, he'd received an anonymous tip that Braxton Brattley was "misappropriating" school funds. *Misappropriating* was a fancy word for stealing. So now Braxton was on probation.

I wondered, who ratted him out?

Maybe I'll send him a muffin basket. Or maybe not.

I☆I☆I☆I

Down in the family room, finally out of bed, I was dressed in pajamas with a sweatshirt over the top, two pairs of socks, and fuzzy slippers. I wasn't cold, but

Mom had turned into her superhero alter ego, Over-protective Mom.

"DAD!" I whined. More like rasped, with my scratchy-sounding voice.

"Jean!" my dad said to my mom. "Give her some room. And maybe she doesn't have to wear two pairs of socks AND the slippers."

I sank down on the deep cushions of the sectional and read Mr. G.'s e-mail for like the eleven hundredth time. The stuff about Braxton I got; but the business about the fund-raising idea, that was still fuzzy.

Then I heard the kitchen door open. Next thing I knew, footsteps came racing from around the corner.

"Bree-Bree! Bree-Bree! Bree-Bree!" shouted Liam. My father tried to catch him by the coat, but the little squirt was too fast. Liam flung himself against me, burying his face into my neck. I could smell the cold air from outside on his clothes, could almost taste the sun-shine on his moon-pie cheeks. He was delicious!

"Bree-Bree, guess what?" He slid off me just far enough to look in my eyes. His knit cap was navy blue to match the marshmallow-puff jacket he wore.

"Come on, little man," Dad said. "Give her some

space. She's still recovering." My cousin was an excited blur of fast talking and big, dimply smiles. He told me all about his big news—how his teacher was planning to buy a whole box of my cupcakes from Wetzel's.

He grinned. "I told her you were my cousin!"

I couldn't help laughing. I put my arms around him and squeezed.

As the day went on, a constant stream of visitors popped in to check on me. Katy came in, snapped a photo of me with Angel on my chest, and said she was making a poster of it.

"My sister, the heartless mogul, turned into an animal lover. Yes, my work here is done. Thank you, thank you!"

When Sara and Becks came over, Sara hugged me and said, "Sweetie pie, we've got your back, all the way!"

She and Becks told me that after Mrs. Benson from the Henry Ford Museum called the DIA, they had been able to set my idea in motion.

When I stared at them blankly, they misunderstood at first.

"Oh, don't worry, Bree. We know how you like

to do things a certain way. So we followed all of your instructions. Soon as you come back to school, you'll be back in charge," Becks said from the doorway. She was scared I might be contagious, even though my dad told her I was cootie free. You can't catch dehydration, anyway. But like I said, Becks had always been a little paranoid about germs.

"Do what a certain way?"

Sara finally realized I had no idea what she meant. She grabbed my clipboard and flipped back several sheets. "Your dad said you must've come up with this just before you conked out," she said, showing me the date next to some scrawly-looking handwriting. "You don't remember?"

Daddy stuck his head into the room and said, "When you should have been passed out from being pumped full of fluids, you somehow managed to make a phone call. You called Mrs. Benson, the woman from the Henry Ford Museum. She called the Detroit Institute of Arts and they ultimately called your teacher."

Sara picked up the story. "Your idea is genius!"

I squinted, reading the clipboard.

Old-School babysitting

What if we hold a massive babysitting service for all the people going to the Old-School concert?

Try to get a venue to donate their space, like Henry Ford or DIA. (DIA better because it's so close to where concert is being held.)

Contact all the elementary schools with little kids who'd need babysitting.

Kids must be at least four, no more than ten years old.

Concert starts at 8. We could keep them from 6 p.m. to 7 a.m.

Kids must bring sleeping bags. Will be separated according to age group.

Ask Mr. G. a fair price to charge for the service.

Only have a few weeks to pull this together. Set up way to take early registration and payment. Online?

Then the memory came back. Me with my voice all scratchy and hoarse on Monday when I'd stayed home sick, calling the museum lady from Henry Ford. I laughed to myself. The cat was sitting on my chest when I called her. The memory was getting clearer. Then I turned to Sara.

"And this is what you guys have been working on all week?" I asked.

"Sweetie, they've been working like dogs," said Becks.

"Does Mr. G. really think we'll be able to raise enough money to make the trip happen?" I asked, turning back to her.

She nodded.

"He thinks it could be our biggest moneymaker ever. But Bree, there's still A LOT to do. So get better soon."

I couldn't help feeling a huge dose of love for my friends. To do this, to work this hard, it made whatever we'd been upset about before seem stupid.

That's what it meant to have friends, I told myself. When you really need help, true friends are the ones who show up.

Civics Journal
Ancient Rome and Middle School

Did you know that in ancient Rome, bathing was a social activity? Like, there were plays and music and exercise areas called palaestra. The bathhouses even had heated floors.

They were sort of like spas today. You know? Except, without the bleach. But just think about it—that junk was nasty! People sitting in the same warm water all day.

Still, the idea of warm baths helping you feel better must've stuck around, because I was all pickle-skinned from so many baths.

But I did feel a lot better.

11

Roman Holiday

Saturday, November 22

I came to the Detroit Institute of Arts for the first time when I was about four. I thought it was the most amazing place in the whole wide world.

Going there made me feel grown-up and special. Nanny (that's what I called my grandma Diane) brought me with her as a special treat. That was long before we knew she was ill, back when Grandpa was still with the Detroit Police Department.

Mom and Daddy had tried convincing Nanny that I would get bored. "She's too young to appreciate most of it," they said.

But Nanny disagreed. "Not my Brianna," she told them. She always treated me like she believed I could do anything. It made it easy for me to believe it, too. Nanny and I took our time, going from room to room. We each had our favorites and we started coming back again and again.

Now, as I walked into the museum, Nanny's rose-scented perfume hit me in the face. I knew it wasn't really her, just the memory of it. Still, my chest tightened, squeezing all the air out of my heart.

I swallowed hard and did a slow turn. So much time had passed since she died and I stopped coming here.

That first time with her was magical, though. Entering each room felt like walking inside a gigantic storybook. The paintings looked like huge illustrations and I would make up stories for each one.

My favorite piece of art was by an artist that Nanny said was "a local success story." Charles McGee, one of our own. I knew when she said that, she meant he was African American, like us. Nanny had light beige skin, and hair that was more red than brown. Cinnamon freckles sprinkled over her nose and cheeks, and her eyes were such a pale gray that they looked almost blue. But she was a "proud black woman from the South." That was how she always said it. She took pride in bringing me to the museum, exposing me to art by all kinds of people, but especially the African American artists. She wanted to make sure I could rock the whole Black Pride thing when I grew up. Living in Detroit, you gotta represent.

When Nanny died, I was seven. Now, as I stood before the enormous painting by Mr. McGee, *Noah's Ark: Genesis*, I shivered. The scene in the painting was shown with all kinds of materials, like rope and cloth, that made you just want to touch it. But I didn't. Even as I reached out toward it, I knew I wasn't going to lay a finger on it. Nanny would come back from her grave, smack my butt with her shoe, then go right on back to heaven.

I remembered how important the collage painting had been to me then. How I used to come to painting and drawing classes here with Nanny and pledged to grow up to be an artist one day. Nanny died a few years later, but until then, I'd been convinced. But at some point, I stopped coming.

Laughter floated up the gallery steps and my thoughts came back to the present. I had come up with an activity plan based on McGee's artwork. I was going to have the kids re-create the painting. Then we would give away goofy, silly prizes.

"Right this way, Miss Justice," said Mr. Prigg. He was the educational coordinator with the museum, tall with long legs, and a long, flat nose, and glasses with rectangular lenses. Mr. Prigg talked with the kind of accent that made you think of snooty people on TV shows.

I'd spent way too much time with Mr. Prigg over the past several days. Setting up the event meant lots of coordination and paperwork. Mr. G. and Principal Striker had practically signed their lives away, promising we wouldn't ruin the museum.

I wouldn't admit it to Mom and Daddy, but I felt lots of pressure to make sure that nothing went wrong. Mr. Prigg's eyes darted from one piece of art to the next, occasionally flicking a gaze back to me. His expression was clear: "Kid, don't mess up my museum!"

So I swallowed hard as we descended to the lower level, where the kids would actually be staying. We turned a corner and the light was cold and gray and felt as far from Charles McGee and the rest of the museum as possible. Chewing the inside of my lip, I told myself to get a grip.

"I'm so excited and so appreciative of the museum," I said. He didn't seem to care.

He pushed open the door to one of the rooms. Under normal circumstances, it was the area used for teaching classes. The walls separating the room from the next space folded and rolled away. Now the space was huge.

Mr. Prigg pasted a smile on his face that fell slightly in the corners. He wasn't happy about this, at all. At least fifty kids between four and ten were ready to tromp through his museum.

"Oh, my goodness, Brianna!" Becks exclaimed, rushing past Mr. Prigg as he retreated. "You look so tiny. Doesn't she look tiny. You're tiny!" She was talking to me and anyone who'd look at her. I loved her to pieces, but Becks was getting stranger and stranger. But no question she'd worked really hard over the past few weeks—all of us had.

Still, whenever we were around each other, it was

like she was eyeing me all weird. The way you'd look at someone you really didn't like all that well.

Now she'd been making a big deal out of the fact that I'd lost weight while I was sick. Every time she saw me, she said something. What was *that* all about?

"Bree!" Becks said, racing over and lifting me off the ground. She squeezed a little too tight.

Have I mentioned how much I hate being picked up like that?

I decided to ignore her, or at least try.

The closer it got to time for the kids to arrive, the faster my heart beat. Grandpa and one of his friends, also a retired Detroit policeman, were my security. Mom and one of her FBI buddies were also helping out.

Daddy was my on-site medic, in case anybody fell down or just needed a lollipop or someone to chase the monsters out of their sleeping bag. He came up and hugged me around my shoulders.

I hugged him back. "Dad, thank you so much. You and Mom didn't have to give up going to the concert to help. You could have gone and had fun," I said, still unable to believe that they'd given up a super-cool date night to help me.

He shrugged. "You know we wouldn't miss this for the world. Now, take a deep breath, Baby Girl. From now until midnight, it's about to get crazy!"

He was so right.

Our charges began arriving about fifteen minutes before six. Although forty-five kids had been registered early, by seven o'clock the number was up to seventy!

We decided to break the tours into two groups. I went on both and told the children we were doing a special project later, so they needed to pay attention. Back in the main room, we'd divided the space into sections based on age and activities. For the older kids, we had a dance competition and video games. The younger kids started off with a craft project.

"One of my favorite artists is a man named Charles McGee," I told the kids. It was funny, seeing them listen to me like I was a grown-up. Liam especially—he looked at me like he was so proud. I . . . I hadn't expected to feel choked up talking to the kids. Looking at their little faces, seeing them so excited about everything, it really did remind me of those visits back in the day with Nanny.

Later, after our tour, I asked, "Who remembers

the big collage painting upstairs that Mr. McGee did?" Several hands shot up. I told the kids we were going to do our own collages. Becks helped me pass out materials. Across the room, I saw Lauren with the dance competition group. I knew she'd be great with them. Still, I wondered if she should have them lined up that way or if it would be better if she broke them into smaller groups.

Then I looked over and saw Sara with another group of eight-year-olds. They were doing crafts, too. We had about eight teachers and twenty-two sixth graders volunteering. Everybody knew what they were supposed to be doing. But I couldn't help it. I almost gave myself whiplash, looking from one group to the other to try to figure out if everybody was doing everything right—you know? The way I'd written it down for them.

"Bree-Bree, can we start our college?" Liam asked.

"Collage," I corrected. I knew I was making myself crazy.

"Bree-Bree?" Liam said again.

I was so distracted with everything going on elsewhere that I wasn't really paying close attention to what I was doing. My clipboard was in my bag across the room. Maybe if I just went over it again and walked around and made sure everyone was doing what they were supposed to? Would that help me feel calmer?

Liam tugged on my sleeve. "Bree-Bree!"

For days I'd led meetings, sent out e-mails, updated everyone with every detail I could think of. Maybe now was the time to just let everyone do what they needed to do.

I drew a big breath and let it out long and slow. Was it time for me to trust my classmates for once?

"Here, Liam," I said, passing him a bundle of pre-cut rope. "Would you help me pass this around?" His face lit up. Another kid tried to grab the rope and I thought for a second there'd be war—or at least, tug-o'-war. It was clear that Liam was proud of his assignment and eager to show what he could do.

Did the sixth-grade volunteers feel that way, too? And if they didn't do everything perfectly, would that really be the end of the world?

Running my own cupcake empire was one thing, but being a leader for other people was really tough. I was chewing on the inside of my lip, listening to the blare of music coming from all four corners of the gigantic space, when Mr. G. came over and checked on us.

"I think it's going really well," he said.

Scanning the room, seeing all the different groups at play, I let out a huge sigh of relief.

I said, "Me, too."

Sara came over and hugged me. "I'm having so much fun," she said. Then she must have remembered that she was supposed to be cool and tough. So she switched back to her sassy-girl attitude.

She said, "*Guuuuurl!* I can't wait 'til we go shopping on Black Friday. Looking around here at all these kids, I've been thinking about all of my money I've earned looking after my baby cousin. Put that with what I have in the bank and I'm gonna be rich!"

She bounced her shoulders up and down and waved her hands in the air. I felt so good, I waved my hands around, too.

Everything felt so great! Talking about holiday shopping with Sara while our other friends moved through the groups of kids laughing and having a good time. The four of us working together, just like we'd done last year during the class election.

Working so hard to make the fund-raiser a success had brought us closer, I was sure of it. We were going to be just like we used to be.

Civics Journal
Ancient Rome and Middle School

The ancient Romans used to have a lot of celebrations. Festivals were often related to gods and goddesses and considered religious. One festival they had was called the Fornacalia. It celebrated baking. How cool is that?

Ancient Romans were all about giving thanks to their deities—gods or goddesses they worshipped.

Middle school has its gods and goddesses, too. In sixth grade, sadly, too many people want to celebrate Prya and Paisley, the so-called popular chicks who crack on everybody else and make people feel bad about themselves.

What should we call their festival?

Well, according to Google Translate, "fakers" translates to *"subditivus puellae."* (Or something like that.)

Can't you just picture it? "Hey, everybody! Let's get together for the big Sub bash! We'll chew the heads off candy Peeps and insult everybody until the weakest kids cry! Let's play pin the tail on the nerd."

12

Pompeii

Friday, November 28

Sometimes you can want something so much that you honest-to-goodness believe you see it. Right there. In front of you. Like, I thought my life had returned to a fun-filled action/friendship movie: *Adventures of the Forever Girls*.

WRONG!

Turns out, once again life was a horror flick.

And it was called *Sharks at the Mall!*

Our big shopping trip the day after Thanksgiving? The one we'd been waiting on for months? DISASTER! Straight-up horrible.

I thought we were there to hang with one another, pick out gifts, and just have a good time. Well, Becks and Sara had other plans. It was all about bumping into the Peas.

So depressing. One minute, the four of us were all together, laughing and having fun. Next thing I know, Becks was scanning the aisles of the store looking for someone. Turns out, she'd been texting the Peas with our every location like some sort of desperate GPS.

And when they showed up, our annual shopping trip went bad faster than old cupcake batter.

The Peas dragged us into this trendy store where they claimed to "shop all the time." Turned out, they were less interested in fashion and more interested in humiliating Becks and Sara.

They convinced Sara and Becks that all of us should try on the same style of jeans. I was, like, whatever, and I knew Lauren couldn't care less. But Sara and Becks were hanging on to their every word, like the Peas were goddesses of fashion.

On Sara the jeans sagged, you know, in the butt region? And on Becks, the pants made her tummy squish over the top. And their so-called popular friends burst into laughter and took out their phones to get some snaps. It was sooooooooo embarrassing.

Prya and Paisley were like hungry sharks feeding on guppies. And Sara and Becks were going for it. Despite being humiliated in the dressing rooms, they still wanted to follow the Peas around.

Lauren and I had had enough. We did our own thing. Lauren tried to make me feel better, but it wasn't the same. Not like it used to be.

When I got home I felt like I'd been in a ninja death battle with the Grinch.

And it wasn't even the worst thing to happen that week. Nope! The worst was yet to come.

Saturday, November 29

The good news? We made our deadline and reached our fund-raising goal! The trip to D.C. was saved!

Yay, right? So why did I feel so *yuck*?

Back in October, getting to this point was the biggest, most important goal in my world.

Now all I could think about was what was happening to me and my friends.

I had not spoken to Sara or Becks since the whole mall thing. I just couldn't even think about them. Couldn't stop thinking about them, either.

Then I got an unexpected text from Toya, one of the girls from the head-shaving article. She was going to the movies, and asked if I wanted to come. We texted and talked on the phone a few times. It was surprising how well we got along. She was real down-to-earth. Cool.

After texting back and forth, I invited Red, too, and the three of us met at the theater. Red's mother was tall and gorgeous and instantly I knew the gossip about her being a beauty queen was no rumor. She was amazing.

"I'm just going to hang out in the mall while you girls see the movie," she said. The parents had talked and Mrs. Chastain drew the short straw—mall babysitter.

We saw a movie that was supposed to be scary, but was more funny than frightening. In fact, we laughed a lot. When it was over, Mrs. Chastain bought us burgers. It was weird—I realized this was the first time I could remember ever hanging out without Sara, Lauren, or Becks.

Much as they were making me crazy, I wasn't ready to just forget about our friendship. When people you cared about were in trouble, didn't you have a duty to stand by them and help them see the mistakes they were making? Wasn't that what being a good leader was all about?

Still, I couldn't deny that listening to Toya talk in a fake British accent while placing her finger over her lip for a mustache, and listening to Red complain about how her ballet teacher was like an evil spirit from a horror movie, was, well, nice. Really, really nice.

Red said, "So you heard about that Braxton kid gettin' in all sorts of trouble?"

"Yeah," I said. "I heard."

We quickly brought Toya up to speed on Braxton Brattley.

Toya said her school had its own Brattleys. And soon we were talking about other things. It was good to put the Brattleys out of my mind. We all went and stood outside, dancing around, laughing like preschoolers, and catching snowflakes on our tongues.

Monday, December 1

I sent Sara a text before first period. We met at the bottom of the steps in the music hall, where Sara had chorus first hour.

"So..." I felt awkward. I didn't know what to say.

She gave a nervous smile. "Don't be mad, Brianna," she finally said.

"I'm not mad," I lied. "I just want to know what's up with you two."

Today she was dressed like an extra from a rap video. Black leather jacket. Black jeans.

I thought back to that day in downtown Detroit, when I was watching all the young businesswomen with their cool business vibe. Since then, I'd toned down my jelly-bean couture. Maybe I should cut her some slack. Maybe Sara was searching for her right look, too.

Without looking up, she said, "Prya said maybe you're just, you know, mad because you want to boss us around. Like maybe you're jealous of them."

It was like being punched right in my gut.

"What?"

When she looked up, a tear clung to her smudgy mascara lashes.

"They're really cool, Bree. You know, popular. Just because that's not important to you, well, it is to us." When she spoke, her voice was shaky. Sara looked away. When she looked at me again, her eyes were smeared where she'd wiped the tear away. When she finished, I was shaky.

"Oh, by the way, Becks wanted me to tell you that we...we're going to switch rooms for D.C. We want to room with Prya and Paisley. Don't be mad. Okay, Bree-Bree?"

They were dumping me? For the Peas? My body felt numb, and I had to bite my lip to keep from saying something really foul. Sara was still talking to me, but I had to walk away.

Sunday, December 7

I was still churning over the whole thing with Sara and Becks several days later when, after church, my parents and Aunt Tina took us to dinner.

Chili's is my favorite restaurant. Their chicken nachos are AMAZING.

While I was chowing down, Aunt Tina, who is the one who got me into saving money when I was little, said it was time I learned how to spend a little of that cash on myself.

"What about your hair?" she suggested.

"What about it?" I was suspicious about where the conversation was going.

She continued, "It's fine, I mean, nothing's wrong with it, but it's the same style you wore in grade school. Don't you think it's time to try something new?"

"I didn't wear it pulled back like this in grade school," I said. My thick curls were held with a band at the back of my head.

She rolled her eyes. "I think it's time for a change."

A change.

I was sick of people talking about change.

And yet...

While we were shopping, I couldn't help feeling a little bit of change going on.

I☆I☆I☆I

What is it about new clothes that make you start imagining yourself as a new person?

Mom and Aunt Tina were like maniacs, pulling all kinds of outfits off the racks for me to try on. Colorful skirts. Bright sweaters. Black tights. Little black boots. Jeans, blouses, T-shirts with snarky sayings. Belts and necklaces.

Aunt Tina picked up this purse that was extremely expensive. "Baby Girl, this would be a great bag for you. You're a little businesswoman now. You need something like this!"

The price tag was CRAZY. She said it was a designer bag. From somebody called Coach. I said for that kind of money, it should be called the Whole Team.

Even though I was tired of Mom, Katy, and Aunt Tina treating me like some tween Barbie doll...I had to admit, trying on all those clothes was kinda nice.

Because here's the thing. I mostly wear jeans, tees, and hoodies. I like my clothes comfy and bright. I always thought girls who wore outfits with little skirts and black tights and matching purses and all that...I thought they were, you know, different from me. Not better, not worse, just...not me. I didn't really see myself that way.

You know? Stylish or whatever. And I was totally fine with that.

Except...

I couldn't help thinking about the cool biz vibe those ladies were kicking downtown. You know? That day I ran away and went crazy. Anyway, I had to admit that sometimes clothing does matter, especially if you want people to think about you a certain way. Like, take you seriously and stuff.

And I'd be totally lying if I didn't admit that sometimes I did wonder what it would be like to look...stylish. To feel a little glamorous.

So when Mom and Aunt Tina and Katy insisted that I let them buy me skirts and blazers and little boots, tights and necklaces and jeans that were not candy-colored, I let them.

Later, as I tried to fall asleep, it was hard to get the memory of my reflection out of my head. When I saw myself, it was me, only not *me*. Is that weird? It felt weird.

"You're going down there to learn about being a leader. I think it's time you put on your big-girl shoes," Aunt Tina had said.

Huh?

"You're becoming a lady now, Brianna," she said. "It's time to know the difference between shoes you can bum around in"—she glanced at my high-tops—"and shoes you wear into battle!"

Into battle?

She and Mom had giggled like chickens. Mom said, "Sometimes we have to go in and make an impression. We have to stand up and fight for something. Whether it's fair or not, the difference between winning and losing can come down to how we present ourselves."

I couldn't stop thinking of those women downtown. Maybe Mom and Aunt Tina had a point, after all.

Civics Journal
Ancient Rome and Middle School

We watched a movie in class called *Pompeii*. It's about this city in ancient Rome that was destroyed by a volcano. Mr. G. explained later that when historians studied Pompeii, they discovered entire meals still sitting inside ovens or on dinner tables, covered in ash. That means that the volcano struck so quickly, people barely had time to do anything before they were just...gone!

So that got me to thinking:

How does middle school life compare to Pompeii? Hmm...

Well, for one thing, change is sort of like that volcano. Both can strike when you least expect it.

And in an instant, nothing is the same.

13

Horatius at the Bridge

Monday, December 8

Our buses, their sleek bodies trembling in the parking lot behind the school, looked a little like monsters. You know? Exhaust curling in the early-morning air, looking like smoke rings from some ancient creature. It felt out of this world.

Or maybe I just wanted to believe it was another world because I was feeling so weird and alien.

It should have been the happiest morning EVER! *I DID IT! We did it!* We raised all the money we needed and still had some to spare. I was going to get the chance I'd been praying for—a chance to meet the editors of *Executive,*

Jr. face-to-face. A chance to learn how to grow my business and become a butt-kicking leader. Everything I ever wanted. And all of my friends were coming, too.

Only, Sara and Becks didn't want to be my friends. They'd made that clear. Just thinking about it made me feel sick inside. Lauren and I had been forced to find two other people to room with. Red volunteered, which was okay, I guess. Then one of the girls who'd helped with the cupcakes, Ebony, became our fourth.

Not Becks.

Not Sara.

Not that having only Lauren left from my old group was bad. Lauren was cool and all, but it had always been the four of us. With Sara and Becks dissing me, I felt lonely inside.

"You gonna be all right, Peanut?" asked Dad. He had driven Mom and me to the school. I tried to give him a *whatever* shrug, but he knew when I was blowing him off. He continued to give me that worried Dad look until Mom opened her door.

"Come on, sweetie," she said. "We'd better get going."

I started to slide across the seat, pushing open the door, when Dad caught my arm.

"Brianna," he said. I hesitated, and he went on. "You're gonna be just fine, baby. Believe that."

As if on cue, the opening notes to another song filled the car, and it was enough to lift me out of my funk, for the moment at least. I gave my father a playful punch. "Yeah, yeah, yeah," I said, smiling. " 'Cause I'm awesome like that."

"You're dang right you're awesome. Go! Get outta my car, brat. Have a great trip!"

I shut my door, let out a long, shaky breath, and headed to the bus. Right about now I should've been experiencing the nervous energy I get when it's time for a field trip. About to miss several days of school, going to a new city, wearing new field-trip clothes—awesome, right?

Instead, something cold and heavy weighed against my chest. Was it dread? A broken heart? Gas?

Or was it loneliness weighing me down?

I☆I☆I☆I

We still had about twenty minutes to go before we left, so the bus was less than half-full.

"Hey, girl!" A hand shot up. I worked really hard to

make my smile look convincing. It felt broken, though, hanging limply on my face.

"Hey, Red, what up?"

Because she was Red and Red was crazy, she couldn't help herself, even at that early hour. She made kissy sounds and her eyes got big and round.

"Ooooo! Look at your hair. It's all swingy and purdy!" she said.

Aunt Tina had talked me into getting something called a blowout. That blow-dryer in the salon was hotter than Satan's tanning bed. Now, instead of bouncy curls that snapped up around my shoulders, my hair stretched straight down the middle of my back. It felt weird, having my hair blowing in the wind like that.

"Thanks," I said. "Gotta get used to it. With my hair fluffy, I think it kept my ears warm. But now…"

"It's so cold outside. Wonder if this is what it feels like inside my ballet teacher's heart."

Okay, Red was funny, in a dark comedy sorta way. "I thought you told me your ballet teacher was heartless," I said, pushing my bag under the seat and climbing in next to the window. She'd already told me she was not a window seat kind of girl.

"Heartless...frozen heart? It's a fine line," she said, easing back her seat. "You okay?"

Shrug. "Just awesome," I said, mimicking her *ouuuuuuusome* tone from the first day we met.

After that, the whole woe-is-me act left me feeling sick of myself. I hadn't really gotten over anything, but I couldn't just sit around moping. I hated that mess. So I decided to at least act like I had some sense.

Red and I joked around about who was going to be overdressed for the trip and who'd wear too much makeup trying to look older. We wondered which of her many cardigans Mrs. G. would wear in her official capacity as chaperone.

Click boarded the bus a little while later. He looked half-asleep, but when he saw us, his face broke into a wide grin. He sat in the seat in front of us, but turned around on his knees to show us the screen on his camera.

"Oh! You put it all together!" I squealed. We'd done a movie this time about kids on a bus trip. I'd helped him set up the shots and move the figures. But I hadn't seen it all put together.

He adjusted the camera so we could see the finished project. When it was over, we cheered and Click beamed. Red said, "It amazes me how you guys do those little movies. It's so cool."

Another boy leaning over Click's shoulder said, "Now *that's* what's up!" We all laughed. Click reached inside his bag and pulled out a sketchbook.

"What's this?" I asked as he handed it over the seat to me.

He grinned. *Click-click!* In addition to being a mini-film maker, Click was an excellent artist.

"That's so cool!" Red said, pointing at the pages. Click did a little bow in my direction as I read the title.

The Adventures of Cupcake Girl!

I flipped through the pages and laughed harder and harder. A cupcake crusader for justice—now that's really what's up. "Click, you could not have done a better job. Thank you!"

Click-click.

His cheeks reddened. "Wish I had known you were changing your hair. I would have made her look a little different," he said, glancing at my blown-out do.

As the buses filled, the party atmosphere grew. Everybody had something to say about my hair. Ebony boarded the bus wearing a navy-and-white scarf wrapped around her head.

"Just got my hair done," she said, plopping down next to Lauren, who was across the aisle from me and Red. "Gotta keep it pinned up 'cause I know I'm going to sleep on this bus." Then, as if to prove the point, she let out a long yawn. She looked over at me and her eyes popped out. Then she was, like, "Girl, you need a scarf!" And she handed me one out of her bag that still had the tag on it. Aunt Tina was right. Black girls have to learn how to protect their 'dos.

We were all laughing and joking and having a good time. At least, until I looked out the window and into the second bus. I saw Mrs. G. talking to someone. When she moved, all the laughter drained out of me.

It was Becks, and Sara was standing right behind her. Prya and Paisley were with them. It was easy to see that the Peas were in control, that Becks and Sara were following them around like puppies.

Why couldn't they see what was going on with

those girls? What was it about the Peas that made my friends like them . . . like them better than me?

It just didn't make any sense.

I☆I☆I☆I

It was five thirty in the morning. We'd been rolling along for about half an hour. I poked my earbuds into my ears and cranked up my playlist. After seeing Becks and Sara with their new besties, I just needed to drift away. Darkness settled in around the outsides of the bus. Already most of the kids who'd gotten on making noise and grinning ear to ear were sleeping—some even snoring. Mom was sitting two rows behind the bus driver next to another parent, way ahead of where we were sitting.

Red stretched her leg, pointed her toes, and reached her foot toward the ceiling of the bus. I yanked one earbud free and looked at her.

She eyed me back and said, "What?"

"Do you want to be a ballerina when you grow up? Can you make a living at it? How much money do ballerinas make?" I sat up, pulling the other earbud free, too. Red's blue eyes flashed like jewels. She always wore that thick black eyeliner and her signature black clothes. Always tried so hard to look tough. That was why the whole ballerina thing still threw me for a loop. Looking at her in the bus's dim light, though, I thought her face looked soft. Pretty.

She laughed. "You ask a lot of questions."

I shrugged. "Just curious. I never took dance when I was little. I was more into sports."

"And cooking?"

"That came later."

"So you didn't always want to be a mega-millionaire with a cooking show or whatever?"

I sighed.

"I do care about things besides money," I heard myself say.

She turned to face me. I could see the streetlamps along I-75 reflected in her gaze. "Hey, I know I haven't known you very long, but one thing I do know is you talk about your future, like, all the time. Gotta admit, sometimes it's pretty annoying."

"Um, thanks?"

"No, I mean . . . well, yeah, I won't deny it. Sometimes I'm, like, 'That girl needs to give it a rest!' But I gotta hand it to you, Justice, when you commit to something, you really commit. At least with you, it's not so much that you talk about money, you talk about success. Most kids think the two are the same. But I can appreciate the hard work you put into everything. You're cool like that."

At the same exact time we both crisscrossed our legs and tucked them beneath us on the seats. Then we laughed.

My smile disappeared, though.

My tone grew serious. "I used to be so sure of myself. So sure of what I wanted," I said. "But since coming to middle school, it's like so much has gotten turned upside down."

Red was nodding. "Tell me about it," she said. "I know exactly how you feel."

I kept going. "In elementary school, I had never thought about journalism. Becks, my..." I caught myself. What was she now? Still my friend? "I mean, Becks was the writer in our group. She wanted to be a novelist. Travel the world. Maybe be a reporter, too. Not me. I Googled *journalists* when we were working on a project in fifth grade. Most of them do not become millionaires."

"So you never wanted to be a journalist."

"That's just it. Now, I don't know. Maybe. I like it—a lot. Mrs. G. is an excellent teacher. When she talks about the power of the press, I don't know, it makes me wonder if that might be something I would love to be part of."

"What's wrong with that?"

"Nothing, except I've been going on and on for so long about being a baker and a millionaire, so I feel like that's what people expect from me. Sometimes I feel...trapped. You wouldn't understand." I blew out a huge sigh.

"Understand what?"

I lowered my voice. "Lately, I feel like I'm pretending all the time."

Lowering my head, I practically whispered, "Want to know the truth, Red? Sara and Becks have been driving me insane! I love them, but the longer we're in middle school, the more I'm starting to feel like we don't have as much in common. They were my best friends

184

because they'd always been my best friends. But... I don't know."

She gave me a look. "You think I don't know anything about fakery? Wake up, Justice!"

I shushed her because her voice rose. Lauren, who was dozing across the aisle, sat up.

"What's up, you guys?" she asked.

"Nothing, Lauren. Go back to sleep."

A minute or so later, Red whispered, "Look around, Justice. I'm a redheaded white chick in a predominantly black city at a predominantly black middle school. I dress like a goth and hide ballet slippers in my book bag. And you think you're the only one who feels like a fake?"

We both sat in silence for a bit after that. It was after seven before Red and I said anything else.

I said, "You never answered my question."

"What question?"

"Do you want to be a ballerina when you grow up?"

She smiled a little smile. "I don't think about it, really," she said.

"Why not?"

"I told you before that I'd been dancing for nine years, but not exactly consecutively."

"Why not?"

She took a long pause. Finally, she answered.

"I was born with a rare heart disease. Started having heart surgeries when I was still a baby."

I could feel my eyes bulging.

"Don't go all dramatic on me, Justice. Spoiler alert—I survive!"

We both laughed. Then she looked around to make sure no one was paying us any attention, then reached down and pulled back the collar of her shirt. A thin pink scar zigzagged across her pale skin.

"Does it hurt?"

"Don't be lame." She laughed. "It doesn't hurt. At least, not anymore. I started dancing when I was really young, about three. By then I was healing and getting healthy and they told my mom I needed to build up my strength. She'd been a dancer, so . . ."

"So she felt comfortable putting you in dance."

"Exactly. And everything was all good, until about two years ago. I came down with pneumonia and the next thing we knew, I was out of school again, undergoing surgeries. I came closer to dying than I ever had."

"God, Red! I'm so sorry!"

Again she paused. Took a breath. Finally, she said, "I'm not. Now, every day that I dance feels like a victory. I don't think about being a ballerina when I grow up. Dancing makes me feel alive—it's like celebrating that my heart is healthy. So I don't do it because it might turn into a career. I do it because it's like my way of being grateful. Ballet is what I love to do. When we read that story in the *Free Press* about Lacy and her friends, it really touched me. I wish I'd had friends like that when I needed them."

It was my turn to be quiet for a bit. I reached over and squeezed her hand. "Well, you've got a friend like that now."

Red leaned back against the headrest. "You know, I'm only on this bus, going to this conference, because you made it seem so do-or-die. I mean, you are truly committed. My ballet teacher freaked when she found out I'd be gone for a few days."

"Why?"

She turned in her seat and faced me.

"I won the lead role in the *Nutcracker* performance at the Fox Theatre."

"Oh my goodness! What a huge honor!" I practically squealed. "It must feel so good to accomplish something like that."

"After several surgeries and a lot of time alone, tell you what, Justice. It doesn't feel nearly as good as making a friend. So, don't blow it. Now hush up and get to sleep!"

The swoosh of the bus's tires created a soothing rhythm. I drifted away, conscious of one important thing:

The tension that squeezed my insides whenever I thought about Sara and Becks changing, well, it seemed to loosen. For the first time in weeks, I felt like I could breathe just a little bit better.

Civics Journal
Ancient Rome and Middle School

One of my favorite myths out of ancient Rome is "Horatius at the Bridge." Horatius was a soldier when Tarquin the Proud was king. Good ol' Tarquin was the last king of Rome and he was terrible.

When the Romans ran his butt outta town and across the Tiber River bridge, Tarquin tried to fight his way back.

If it hadn't been for Horatius fighting alone, Tarquin may have retaken control of Rome.

I've been feeling like that—like I'm fighting the enemy on my own.

The Peas and the rest of the so-called populars are like Tarquin—trying to fight their way on top when they should be driven out of the city. Or at least the middle school hierarchy. What I'm saying is in middle school, you have to dig deep and find your inner Horatius, because there'll always be a Tarquin trying to push you aside. Rip down that bridge, baby. Keep Tarquin out!

14

SPQR

The lobby appeared to reach all the way to heaven.

We had taken an escalator up from the ground floor. Pale shades of gold and cream covered the walls, the furniture, the carpets and tiles. The hotel's ceiling was a lacework of glass and snow-white iron beams.

I couldn't believe these hotel people were letting a bunch of kids invade their nice space. If Mr. G. and Principal Striker had to pay a deposit, we might get sued out of our school and have to hold classes at the National Guard Armory back home!

Of course, we weren't the only sixth graders.

Through the floor-to-ceiling windows we watched dozens of kids huddled together, laughing and running along the sidewalks. It wasn't nearly as cold in D.C. as it had been in Detroit. No snow on the ground. A toasty warm forty-three degrees, we'd heard the bus driver say as he was parking.

Mr. G. and my mom went to the check-in counter while we stood behind a wall of teachers and other chaperones.

"Oh, Lordy! Brianna, this place is amazing. Are you responsible for this?" Red looked impressed and mischievous at the same time. Light spilled from the glittering chandeliers and lit her red hair like a flame. I self-consciously tossed my own hair over my shoulder, still not used to it being all loose and swingy.

"Well, of course. Because I'm classy and I demand classiness wherever I go!" I said.

"So, that's a no, then," Red said, giving me a shove to the shoulder. We did our best to wander away from the herd (despite being specifically warned not to wander away from the herd). In front of us was a small staircase, and at the foot of the stairs were these creamy white cards, large like poster board, but much more elegant.

Each card sat in a brass holder that stood about three feet high. And each card featured elaborate golden cursive writing.

The Gemstone Society Show
Mezzanine Level

Clockmakers of America
Ballroom G

Handmade Doll Craft Association
The Neptune Room

Welcome!
Leadership Conference USA
and All Class Presidents
Opening Reception at 4 p.m.
The Coral Room

I knew it was probably dorky, but a chill ran through me as I read the welcome card. Red whipped out a camera and we went into a selfie frenzy.

But before we could sneak back to the group, I was totally busted. A huge man wearing a white chef's hat and apron came out of nowhere, shouting my name.

"BRIANNA! LOOK AT YOU!" He was darker than dark roast coffee.

Lauren bent down and whispered, "You know him, Bree?"

"Uncle Al?" I said, squinting up at the man. By then Mom and Mr. G. had returned to our group. Of course, all the kids who had been minding their own business were now all up in mine.

"Al!" said Mom, going on tiptoe to hug her brother-in-law.

"How'ya doing, girl!" he boomed, lifting her into the air and twirling her around.

Okay, as much as I hated to have that done to me, I had to admit, it was fun watching Mom spin like a pinwheel. I watched the faces of the other kids and I saw that it seemed to make them happy, too. Was this how people looked at me when other kids were spinning me around? I mean, it was still beyond annoying, but maybe it wasn't the worst thing in the world.

Mom said, "It's so good to see you, Al. We brought you a little baker!" Mom patted Al's thick arm and he gently placed her back on the floor. She waved me over and said, "Brianna, you remember your uncle Al, right?"

He bent down in front of me. His eyes were milk-chocolate soft.

"Oh, child!" he exclaimed. He reached out and took my hand. His thick fingers closed over mine, his palms swallowing my hand like oven mitts. "You really are a sight for sore eyes. What a beautiful girl. You better be glad your mama is a looker, 'cause your daddy is the funniest-looking thing this side of the Mississippi!

"I've got recipes that will blow your mind. Just come across the street to my restaurant, the Kitchen, and see me when you're ready," he said.

Mr. G. called everyone's attention as Uncle Al made his way back across the lobby. We got our room assignments and were given an itinerary—a schedule of what we were going to be doing over the next several days.

Our opening ceremony was in the Coral Room.

That was when they would introduce all of the class presidents.

Lost in thought about my upcoming speech, I felt a tug on the back of my jacket and turned.

I was shocked to see who was standing there. And wearing a super-serious expression.

Beau Brattley.

"Brianna, we need to talk! Like, right now!"

I took a deep breath and remembered my new vow to stay calm and upbeat. Not fake, but mature and leadershippy.

"Hey, Beau, did you have fun on the bus ride?"

He looked at me like I had two heads AND a tail. Okay, so much for small talk.

"Look, Brianna, I just need to tell you something about your friends Sara and Becks," he said.

My heart flipped. I knew I was supposed to be mad at them or whatever, but swear to goodness, if he started ragging on them, I was about to go off.

"What?"

He pulled me away from the group. When we were closer to the floor-to-ceiling windows facing the street, he leaned in and practically whispered:

"Those chicks they're hanging around with, the Peas, they're just using your friends."

I scowled. Outside, the sidewalks were filled with students, the scene playful and wintry, like a snow scene from a video game with very high pixels. Inside, I was whispering like a spy, all hunched over and conspiratorial like I was trading top secret recipes with a rival government chef.

"What are you talking about?" I said. Ghostly fog whirled against the cool window.

Mr. G. looked over in our direction. We both ducked our heads. We heard him say, "If at any point anyone decides to make a moose call or any other sound that isn't *yes, ma'am* or *yes, sir*, we will send you home immediately, per the agreement we have with each and every one of your parents."

Beau Brattley hissed, "Look, it's none of my business, okay. But I just thought you'd want to know. I know for a fact that the only reason Prya and Paisley wanted Tweedledee and Tweedledum to room with them is because they're planning to trick them out of their savings . . . or something like that. Didn't the four of you used to save money together?"

I nodded.

He continued, "Once they get the two of them to spend as much money on them as possible, then they're going to try to humiliate them and get them in trouble."

My face flamed hot. I knew those girls were up to something. She-devils—absolute she-devils!

"Why are you telling me this? Why not tell them?"

It was a fair question. He shifted from foot to foot. When he looked at me, his eyes darted back and forth. Definitely spy material. Maybe D.C. was making us paranoid.

"Okay, here's the thing. I know my brother has been giving you a hard time about the whole president thing, but the truth is, I never even wanted to be president. I just..." He looked at his shoes for a minute. Then he looked at me and gave me a mischievous grin.

"That's why I sent that e-mail to Principal Striker. Someone had to shut my brother down. Using class funds to buy junk for his weird little science experiments. He's trying to be like some evil science genius. I did not want to be president, but he kept trying to drag me into it just for some kind of power trip."

"So you blabbed on your own brother?" I said, incredulous.

His cheeks turned bright pink. "I had to! He was out of control!" His voice squeaked, then he lowered his pitch. "Anyway, whatever. I know they're your friends and I know those girls are up to no good. That Bakari dude, too. Anyway, that's all."

He looked both ways, then started to walk away. He stopped short and looked back. "Oh, and good luck with your speech and everything."

And he was gone.

"So what was that about?" asked Lauren when I returned to the group.

I just shook my head. "Tell you later," I said.

This was just great. Just excellent.

What was I supposed to do? Becks and Sara were both being super-pissy. How was I supposed to save them when they didn't even want to be around me? That was the question.

We found our rooms and were allowed to go in and dump our stuff. I took out my dress for the reception and hung it in the closet. We were supposed to be super-grown-up and elegant.

Mom and Mrs. Garcia, Click's mom, were our chaperones. They got us settled and told us we could go explore the hotel for one hour, but had to come right back.

For the next hour we went up and down the elevators; down and up the escalators. On the mezzanine level, we found the Gemstone Society show. Cases and cases of multicolored gems from deep reds to sparkly clear crystals.

We read the tiny cards that described each piece, but we didn't dare touch anything. Especially since some of the people guarding the gems appeared downright hostile to have sixth graders looking at their stuff.

It was hard to concentrate. Becks and Sara were in trouble. They needed my help. But I didn't know how or what to do. Or if they would even want me to do anything.

Heading down to visit another area, I heard Mom calling my name.

"I have news!" she said, waggling her phone in my direction. When she told me, I couldn't believe it.

"Really? You really did it?"

"Who's the greatest mother in the world?"

"Um..."

She swatted at me, but I ducked in time. All in fun. Then I gave her the biggest hug ever.

"I can't believe you got us into the White House!"

"Well, I already asked for the passes. I could only get four—so I gave them my name, yours, Rebecca's, and Sara's. Tell Lauren I'm so sorry, but I thought if you were trying to mend fences with those two, well..."

"Mom! You're the best. The best best best best!" I hugged her tight.

Lauren would understand. I just knew she would.

I glanced in Red and Lauren's direction. "Let me handle this part," I said. A plan was already forming.

When I told Red, Lauren, and Ebony about my conversation with Beau, they were mixed on whether I should say something. Then I told them my plan.

"You really think that'll work?" Red asked.

I chewed my lip. "I think Becks and Sara are just going through a crazy period. Getting to go to the White House after we visit the Capitol, just hanging out away from the bad influences, it'll make a big difference. I'm sorry. I really wish I had enough passes so we could all go."

Red said, "No worries, Miss J. If you think this'll

help, I say go for it. While you're at the White House hav-ing tea and crumpets with the President, I'll be checking out an exhibit at the National Gallery." She did a first-class ballet twirl and added, "A collection of Degas. He was a master at capturing the art of dance on canvas."

I giggled and did a much less perfect twirl of my own. "Um, first off, Miss Thing, tea and crumpets? He's President, not the queen!"

Red went up on her toes and did a very graceful leap. "And second?" she asked.

"Second off, or secondly, you're ridiculous. But thanks for the support. I really mean it."

Lauren, in her usual easygoing tone, said, "She's right, Bree. It's okay that I'm not going to the White House. I just want you and Becks and Sara to work things out once and for all."

Ebony, however, disagreed. "Well, I think you shouldn't say a thing to them."

"Why?" blurted Lauren.

" 'Cause I think they're doing exactly what they want to do, hanging out with those nasty Peas," she said.

I sighed. Ebony just didn't understand. They were my best friends. As far back as second grade, Becks used to be so awkward. So…needy. Kids picked on her all the time. She was the shyest person I'd ever seen. Always a little, um, heavy, she got teased and called roly-poly. I stood up for her then, and still felt like I had to. And Sara? Always sweet and silly and making us laugh. Thanks to her, we grew up watching *My Little Pony* and giving one another ridiculous horse names.

So it was up to me to help them see what a huge mistake they were making. Before I could explain, however, Lauren jumped in.

"You don't know Brianna that well yet. She's been helping them since we were little kids," Lauren said.

"No offense, Ebony, but Lauren and I know them better than anybody else. Trust me, they don't *really* like those girls; they've just gotten caught up in the whole popular thing."

Ebony snorted. "If you say so, girl."

Guuuurl, I truly do!

I✫I✫I✫I

The afternoon flew by and before we knew it, it was time for the reception. I showered and put on my dress. It was black with burgundy flowers. I wore black tights and tiny black heels with a strap over the top. Mary Janes, Aunt Tina called them.

When we entered the Coral Room of the hotel, a wave of noise washed over us. It was like the cafeteria at school, only it smelled better and all the noise was polite, sort of.

Kids from a few dozen middle schools filled round tables all over the room. We would later learn that most schools brought only a few students. Mr. G. was one of the few teachers crazy enough to try to bring such a huge group.

I was getting nervous thinking about having my name called for recognition. It didn't help any when I saw Sara and the Peas walk in. Where was Becks? For a brief moment, I made eye contact with Sara. I waved and she was about to return the wave when the Peas realized who she was looking at. One of them looked right at me and rolled her eyes. Then she pushed Sara along and made her sit with her back to me. Trolls!

"Good afternoon, and welcome to the twenty-third annual Leadership America Conference," said the man at the podium.

My heart fluttered. All around me kids were snapping photos. Red and Lauren and Ebony, too. The speaker asked for everyone's attention and Mom asked us to all put our phones down.

My moment had arrived. "Now, I'd like to do our annual roll call for sixth- and seventh-grade class presidents," he said. Mr. G. had explained that even though the conference was for both grades, he made a decision to bring only one class. One by one, the speaker called out names from a sheet. Each time, the kid stood and received applause.

When it was my turn, it felt like I was in a movie.

Or maybe a dream.

"...Miss Brianna Justice..."

I stood on shaky knees. It was only for a few seconds, but in that time I glanced around. I saw the smile on Mr. G.'s face and a huge one on my mom's. They looked so proud and it made me feel proud to have their support. All of our students applauded and cheered. Blueberry Hills came to represent! I'm just saying, we rocked it.

The rest of the names floated past in a beautiful ribbon of camera flashes and rippling applause. When he had read the last of the names, the speaker told us to go out and enjoy the reception. He said he'd look forward to seeing some of us in our sessions the following morning. My first session wasn't until Wednesday, so I had all day Tuesday for touring and sightseeing.

"Before I let you all go so you can enjoy lovely finger foods and music, there is one other reminder," said the speaker, his voice bringing my floating heart back to earth. Only, he didn't just bring me down, he crash-landed me into a terrifying heap.

"At the special session, all class presidents are required to participate in our farewell speech. This year's topic is 'Power with a Purpose.' We want you to come up and share with the group how you show your dedication to your community. Each of you will have five minutes. Our partner and one of our sponsors, *Executive, Jr.* magazine, will award prizes to the most innovative speakers and feature them in an upcoming article."

I felt the color rush from my face. What if my speech turned out rotten? I mean, what if it sucked?

"Sugar? You okay?" Red asked as she leaned in.

I whispered, "I'm okay. It's just...being here. It just got real!"

Civics Journal
Ancient Rome and Middle School

After getting rid of their final king, the kingdom of Rome became the Republic of Rome. *SPQR* was stamped on tablets, coins, and everything to show the support of the senate and people of Rome. I think it was sort of like an advertising campaign, to show the countrymen that they were one society.

If middle schoolers made their own coins, what would we stamp on them?

Mine would probably say *COSG*.

That stands for Citizens of Sixth Grade!

It's time for us to stand together and rock this *thang*!

15

Grand Pantheon

Tuesday, December 9

The U.S. Capitol building left me breathless, despite the fact that I hadn't slept well thanks to worrying about my friends—and my speech.

We came in through the visitors' center and had to line up and get name badges. Everyone was whispering or giggling, trying to wake up or calm down. Mr. G. and the rest of the chaperones had on their "don't you embarrass our school, our city, or our state" expressions. Most everybody seemed to understand that they meant business.

"Think you could work in a place like this?" Red whispered.

I whispered back, "It's a lot nicer than holding sixth-grade meetings in the old auditorium at school. That place smells like feet and corn chips."

We both cracked up, but pulled it together when Mr. G. glanced our way.

Once the tour guide arrived, we fell into step behind him. He seemed impossibly chipper for so early in the morning. Focusing on him took my mind off Sara and Becks.

Earlier this morning, while waiting in line for breakfast behind Becks, I'd whispered that I needed to please talk to her and Sara. Alone. Instead of just answering me, she'd written a note:

Meet us behind the Lewis Cass statue @ Capitol building.

Our tour guide had a mustache that danced when he spoke. His eyes were pale blue and his cheeks glowed like Santa's. Swear to goodness, when he laughed, his belly shook like, well, you know the deal. The way he talked about the history of the building and the architecture, you'd think he built it himself.

"Did you know that the original dome of the Capitol in 1824 was made of wood covered with copper?" asked the Santa-looking guide. "By the 1850s, however, that dome was considered a fire hazard. So they set out to improve the old girl. Just one of her many makeovers."

He winked at us and we all laughed. But the snickering and snide comments of my classmates ceased as we climbed the steps and stared into the domed ceiling. We stood, about twenty-five of us, with our mouths hanging open. It was so cool.

We remained speechless in the face of what the guide called "neoclassical design." Our guide said the architect of the U.S. Capitol was a dude named Thomas U. Walter, who'd been inspired by the Panthéon of Paris.

We were in an area called the Rotunda. "This space is the heart of the Capitol building," said the guide. I nudged Lauren and she nudged me back. It was so cool, just being there.

Mr. G. looked like his head was going to explode with joy. The man literally rocked back and forth, even though he must've heard this same speech at least twenty-five times! I wondered if he'd downloaded it onto his iPod.

A "*Pssst!*" jarred me out of thoughts of Mr. G.

I turned in time to see Becks. Her eyes were like huge brown saucers behind her glasses. Sweat dampened my palms. My heart tripped around in my chest, going faster and faster.

I edged away from the group. When I got closer, she shook her head vigorously. I figured out why she'd looked so freaked out.

The Peas!

They'd moved into view. Like buzzards. Both wearing black jackets with some sort of ridiculous feathers around the hoods. Bet if I called animal control, they'd roll in here and shoot the Peas full of tranquilizers. Wonder if I could get that number.

Becks turned. No doubt sensing I might put her precious Peas in danger by calling buzzard tranquilizing authorities. One Pea was saying something to her, face blocked by said hood. Becks's eyes grew extra-large again. She didn't look my way.

"Any questions?" asked the guide. "Now I am

going to lead you into an area that is always a hit with school groups, Statuary Hall."

Red, Lauren, and Ebony were ahead of me. I was hanging back, waiting for Becks. Out of the corner of my eye, I saw Sara snap several photos of Prya and Paisley. It occurred to me that I hadn't seen Sara take one selfie since we left for D.C.

The guide was leading us through a hallway from the Rotunda to Statuary Hall when I realized there was something going on at the back of the group. I turned just in time to see Mr. G.'s face flame red.

A man dressed like some kind of guard or police-man was standing there. So were the Peas. I let my eyes drift over to Becks. She looked green. Sara seemed to grow smaller and smaller.

My mom and another teacher turned themselves into curtains, blocking out the drama and directing the rest of us to mind our business and follow the guide and other chaperones.

From somewhere on a lower level a door opened and a gust of bitter cold rushed in and nipped at my ankles.

"*Pssst!*" Becks hissed, sounding like an angry teakettle. She and Sara stood together. The Peas were being led in the opposite direction.

This time when I looked back, Becks was using her head to point to the rear of the gallery, a space filled with statues. We had learned earlier that each state donated two statues, most of which were located in other parts of the building. The rest gathered here, motionless, as though all had been in the middle of some great presentation when they simply froze for all eternity. A shiver skittered through me. Would I wind up like them during the closing session? Frozen in time when I couldn't come up with a decent presentation for my "Power with a Purpose" speech?

While the guide pulled the group toward one side of the space, Becks, Sara, and I wound up on the opposite side of the room. Just like she'd said in the note, we were behind a statue of Lewis Cass.

"Is this the dude they named Cass Tech after?" I asked, squinting up at the huge white statue. Cass Technical High School was one of the best schools in Detroit. I tried not to notice that Becks was looking like she couldn't care less.

She jumped right in. "Why do you want to talk to us so bad?"

Sara glanced all around. She looked tired.

"You know, the Peas know you don't like them. If you keep bothering us, they're not going to let us hang out with them," Sara said.

"What?" I felt off balance. I looked at her—really looked at her. Her hair was frizzy. Her clothes were rumpled.

"And what's wrong with your hair, Sara?" They both looked wrong. Their body language was wrong.

Becks huffed, "Oh? So now, because your aunt got your 'natural' blown out and it's all swishing down your back, you want to make fun of Sara?"

"I'm not making fun of anybody. Why do you have such an attitude? I was just asking a question. And what happened to your little friends, anyway?" My heart was pounding hard and fast. It was like we had never been friends, the way they were pulling away from me. I just wanted to help them.

Why were they making it so hard?

"They got caught with gum, that's all," Becks said defensively.

Now, believe me when I say, we had gone over Capitol Etiquette—an actual pamphlet that Mr. G. made us memorize—for the past month. He must have told us a million times: NO GUM!

I shook my head. "Well, that was stupid. So typical. Anyway, this is cool, right? Lewis Cass. We should take pictures. Sara, are you gonna selfie?"

"Brianna, shut up!" Becks's anger crackled like lightning, its flash so hot and intense that both Sara and I took a step back.

"What did you just say to me?" I asked, trying to regain my balance, feeling shaken.

Sara looked around, then beckoned for us to follow her to another spot. I struggled to get my anger under control. She told me to shut up. I couldn't believe it.

When we were sure we were no longer in a whispering gallery (an area designed to amplify voices even if they whisper), Becks spun around. "Look, Brianna. You don't know them, Prya and Paisley. So why do you always have something to say?!" She was practically panting. Not just in anger. Rage!

Sara wasn't helping. "Look, Brianna, it's nothing against you, okay? It's just, you know, we're hanging with new people now. Don't be mad. You've got that Red girl and your little friend Click. We've got the Peas. Prya and Paisley said when we go to the mall today, they would hook me up with a total makeover. That's why I didn't do much with my hair. Prya said I should wait until she helps me pick out my new clothes, then take a ton of pictures."

Before I even had a chance to think about it, the words shot out of my mouth. "Um, is she going to tell you when to go to the bathroom, too?"

I blew out a large sigh. "Sorry," I said. "Look, I wanted to talk to you because Beau Brattley told me something. He said the Peas are planning to trick you out of your money. They're just hanging with you guys to try to get free stuff. Hey, I'm sorry, but they're not good people. I was trying to find a nice way to say it, but, whatever. Anyway, don't sweat it. If you're scared of telling them where to go, please let me. I've had it with them bossing you guys around...."

"BEAU BRATTLEY?" This time Becks's voice rose so loud that it didn't take any architectural magic to make it carry. Several people spun around to see what was going on now. We all scooted tighter behind the statue.

Becks pushed her face up close to mine. "Since when do you even care what Beau Brattley thinks about anything?"

"Look, he came to me!" I sputtered.

"Then you should tell him to mind his own business!" Becks was definitely panting now. "And by the way, you're just mad because we want to hang with them and not you. If anybody wants to boss us around, it's you, Brianna Justice. You're just not satisfied until you're telling everybody what to do!"

Now I was stammering. "So it's like that, then? You're just going to jump at me like that when I'm trying to do you a favor?"

My heart thumped in my throat. Heat crept into my neck, scalding me. All last night while Uncle Al had been showing me around his kitchen, worrying about the big gathering he was preparing for, all I could think about was these two. But all they'd been thinking about, it seemed, was how to get rid of me. I felt like screaming at them.

Too bad she beat me to it.

"You have a lot of nerve!" she said. Me? More like

her. Talk about nerve! "We told you already, we want to be friends with them. Why are you still bothering us? Do yourself a favor and leave us alone!"

"I..." My anger fizzled into something small and quiet. "I thought you were my friends." I couldn't let them see me cry. I wouldn't.

"Look, we're outta here!" Becks snapped.

"Wait!" I called, my voice soft. I knew I should just shut up, but I felt the words pour out. "Mom got the tickets. For the White House. It was going to be a surprise. I thought...I thought you really wanted to visit the White House."

"You think me and Sara would rather go to the White House with you than to the mall with Prya and the rest of 'em?"

Becks scrunched up her features like she was trying to swallow something bitter. A combination of anger and hurt and something else—something I didn't recognize. Sara's voice was kinder, but she wasn't much better. "No need for everybody to get all worked up. Bree, we can't go to the White House. I'm sorry."

She tugged at Becks's sleeve. The softness of Sara's

voice was way more of a punch than the ugly edge in Becks's. Because Sara sounded like she felt sorry for me. Like I was the one acting pathetic.

Which, let's face it, I was.

There. I'd said it. I, Brianna Justice, president of the whole sixth grade, was pathetic.

Mr. G. called for his students to line up, but I felt more stuck than the statues. I trudged across the polished floor and when I reached my group, I told Lauren, Red, and Ebony what happened.

Ebony was, like, "Girl, I'm sorry and everything, but I tried to tell you it was a bad idea. Those chicks know what they're doing. Mama says sometimes when folks are determined to make mistakes, you just gotta let 'em."

Red gave me a hug. "Don't worry about it, Justice," she said. "It'll be all right."

But it was Lauren who left a giant lump in my throat.

She said, "Brianna, I'm so sorry. I know how much you wanted things to go back to the way they were. I know you're not happy being friends with me without them. I…" She choked up. "I hope you'll still hang out with me anyway."

I'd been so caught up in trying to make Becks and Sara be my friends that I didn't even see how I was brushing Lauren off.

I threw my arms around her. I said, "I'm sorry, Blondie." She grinned. She always laughed when I called her that. "You're my girl, Lauren. I don't need Becks and Sara to still be friends with you."

As soon as I said it, it was like something inside me changed. I knew what I'd just said was true. It was time to start acting like it.

Still, part of me felt so empty. I knew it was the part where Sara and Becks were supposed to be.

I☆I☆I☆I

While most of the students took buses back to the hotel, Mr. G. offered a few of us in the honors class a chance to stay a little longer. I was feeling so pitiful, I couldn't bear the idea of leaving just yet and bumping into the girls again.

Mr. G. took us into the back hallways of the Capitol, introducing us to our congressmen. Then we had the chance of a lifetime, to enter the Senate chamber, where senators conduct important business, deciding all kinds of laws and important stuff for the nation. Any other time, I would have been bug-eyed with excitement. But now my stomach burned as I tried not to throw up. I still felt awful about everything that had happened.

We entered the Senate chamber and took seats up above the area where the senators sat. A woman, tall and curvy, wearing a navy blue pantsuit over a white shirt, had the floor.

Mr. G. leaned in and whispered, "That's Senator Madeline Wilson-Hayes."

At first, I slumped down in my seat. My head buzzed as my mind kept replaying what had happened with Sara and Becks. Still, the richness of the senator's voice, and the way other senators kept trying to cut in while she was talking, well, it got my attention.

After about half an hour, we ducked outside again. In the hallway I asked, "Why were those people yelling at her?"

I could tell he was psyched that I was interested. "That is our adversarial government at work! Senator Wilson-Hayes is trying to make a point about the woeful lack of funding for teaching technology to young students. Since taking office, she has seen it as her pur-pose in life to make sure all students have access to this kind of education."

Her *purpose*. Now my stomach boiled yet again, but for a totally different reason. Despite how bad I felt about fighting with Sara and Becks, I knew that if I didn't come up with a speech about how to have "power with purpose," I was going to feel even worse.

I wished I could run down the steps and ask the senator how she came up with her purpose. Maybe she could help me find mine.

Civics Journal
Ancient Rome and Middle School

The Grand Pantheon was constructed during the Roman Empire. It was to be an offering to the gods.

The Capitol building was definitely a building worthy of them, too. It was grand and beautiful and awe-inspiring.

I don't really know how to connect the Grand Pantheon to middle school, except maybe that the structure has gone through many renovations to meet the needs and beliefs of the citizens as societies have changed.

If a building from thousands of years ago can change and adapt, maybe I can, too.

Would that make me the Grand Pantheon of friendship?

16

The Palace

On the way to the White House, Mom swerved on the ice and we skidded.

"Sorry!"

The roads were getting slicker and snow had begun to fall. Snowflakes slid off the rental car, and immediately turned into ice.

Mom was pretty smart. Didn't take her long to realize there was only one kid rather than the three she'd expected. I'd told her a little bit of what had happened in my latest horror show, *Night of the Living Dead Statuary Hall*! I left out the bits about my utter humiliation.

Still, I think she knew something was wrong. Like, really, *really* wrong.

Even thinking about what happened made me tear up all over again. My so-called friends dissing me like that.

And me, treating poor Lauren like she didn't matter.

I didn't know who I was more sick of—Becks and Sara, or myself for spending so much time trying to win them back that I was neglecting people who actually did like me for me.

My heart twisted. I bit my lips hard and tried not to leak stupid tears all over my newly blown-straight hair.

Mom and I were inching toward the White House, but I couldn't get that image of Sara and Becks running off with Prya and Paisley out of my head.

Remembering the look in their eyes, I thought maybe they had changed more than I'd ever imagined.

Mom lowered the SUV's window to show her ID and badge to the security officer when we finally reached the White House gate. Armed guards walked around our car and slid a giant mirror underneath it that Mom said was to check for bombs. Like a spy movie? Cool, right?

But instead of feeling cool, I was flat-out miserable.

Mom guided the SUV into a parking space, then let out a sigh.

"Look, baby, I know your feelings are hurt and you feel like your friends betrayed you. I get that. But when we get inside, and you meet my good friend Letitia, who moved heaven and earth to make this happen, could you please do your old mom a favor and pretend you're having a good time? For me?"

It took a few seconds of deep breathing and several attempts at swallowing the lump in my throat before I could answer her. The first thought that came to mind was, *Sure, Mom, no problem. I'm an excellent faker.*

Maybe it was time for me to stop worrying so much about faking, and get real about wanting to explore all the possibilities.

"I'm good, Mom," I said with a smile. And I wasn't faking one bit.

I☆I☆I☆I

We were in the White House kitchen. Holy cow! I thought seeing the kitchen at Uncle Al's restaurant was impressive. It was nothing compared to this!

And it turns out I had a lot in common with the First Lady.

Can you believe I just said that?

I'd imagined that when she was in the White House she wore diamonds in her ears and pearls around her neck. I pictured her being all glamorous. Sure, she seemed nice on TV, but when you're married to the President, you sorta have to act that way.

But the First Lady wasn't snooty-acting at all. She wore overalls. Cute overalls, but still, overalls. She wore a pale yellow sweater underneath and plain white Vans sneakers. Made me wish I hadn't taken my aunt's advice and had worn my regular high-tops, rather than these toe-pinching boots. Although, I had to admit, with the pleated skirt and black tights, the leather jacket and raspberry scarf, I did feel kinda sophisticated and cool.

"Come and let me look at you," she said, reaching out for my hand. "My goodness. Such a beautiful young lady." She glanced at Mom and said, "You must be very proud."

Mom smiled her best proud-mama grin, then the First Lady glanced back at me. "Letitia tells me you love to bake and plan to own your own bakery someday."

And before I could stop myself, I blurted, "Well, I do like to bake, but maybe I'll do something else when I grow up, like being a journalist or even an artist! But Miss Delicious says learning good leadership skills prepares you for success in life, so I was hoping to bump into your husband today and get leadership advice."

There was silence.

Mom, Letitia, and the First Lady stared at me. Mom's face was a mixture of alarm and super-duper embarrassment. My eyes went totally huge. I'd just contradicted the First Lady. And I made it look like Miss Letitia didn't know what she was talking about. AND it came out sounding like I didn't care about meeting her—the First Freakin' Lady—because I'd rather meet her husband. *Nice job, Justice.*

So imagine my surprise when everybody started laughing—really, really laughing.

"Sweetheart, I know William is around here somewhere, and if anybody could offer a few tips on leadership, Lord knows it would be him. As for the part about not knowing what you want in life, honey, you've got plenty of time." Her accent was softer than Red's, with a hint of honey.

She slid onto a stool at the large granite counter, getting comfortable. "This is my favorite room in the whole house. Want to know why?"

I nodded. Mom sat down and I perched myself on the stool between them. Miss Letitia stood beside the First Lady, clutching several calendars and day planners. And a clipboard. *Hmm.*

"When I was little, I used to cook with my mama all the time." Her feet barely reached the floor. (Neither did mine.)

"All the while I was growing up, I was convinced I'd be the next great chef. Don't tell anybody." She leaned in like I was her best friend, curling her fingers around mine and making me feel as though we'd known each other forever. I couldn't stop myself from smiling.

"Whenever I get a free moment around here, my favorite way to unwind is to spend time watching the cooking shows on TV. I was beyond devastated when they canceled Miss Delicious's *Delicious Dish*!"

"Me, too!" I cried.

She grinned, squeezing my fingertips. "Anyway, when I was a sophomore in high school, I took an art class. I still remember my teacher's name, Mr. Gasparini. He was a great artist. His passion inspired me. By the time I was a senior, all I could think about was art. So I wound up going to art school. Now, because I'm married to you-know-who, I have the greatest job in the world. I get to be an advocate for arts programs and artists everywhere."

I asked: "Um...ma'am, I mean, Miss First Lady, when you finally realized you loved art more than cooking, did it...I mean, did you feel...I don't know...feel like you were failing? I mean, did it scare you to change your mind?"

Her smile started in her eyes and made her whole face shine. "Of course! Oh, my goodness. It sounds like we're so much alike. I was very determined as a girl. I thought I knew exactly what I wanted. But the more I exposed myself to new things, the less sure I became. It took a while for me to accept that changing my mind could be a good thing."

"Me, too!" I said. Mom just laughed, shaking her head. She was wearing her *Oh, Brianna* face.

And with that, we were off on our tour through the

White House. The First Lady joined us, which none of us expected, and she even let me interview her for our school's blog. Mrs. G. was going to have a heart attack.

The house held so much history. In the Blue Room was an enormous Christmas tree. It was decorated with glittery and glass balls with painted faces and scenes.

"Can you believe it? Sixth graders in Muskegon Heights, Michigan, made those ornaments. They were in danger of losing their art budget, but thanks to our efforts, we were able to save the program for the children." The First Lady grinned. I'd heard of Muskegon. A little town just about as far west of Detroit as you could get without falling into Lake Michigan.

She continued, "Every year that we live here, working with all the volunteers who help make our house come alive at this time of year is one of the biggest honors imaginable." She explained how First Ladies had been coming up with Christmas decorating themes since Jacqueline Kennedy did it in 1961.

"I've heard of her," I said.

She linked her arm with mine. "She was considered one of our most stylish First Ladies, so of course, a young woman of such style would have heard of her!" She winked and I giggled like an idiot. But she didn't seem to mind.

We moved on, soon returning to the kitchen to meet Alexander Quimby, the White House chef. He came over and we talked about recipes.

The First Lady said that in addition to her passion for art, she had a passion for healthy eating. Mr. Quimby told me that the president had a much broader view of what it meant to be healthy and his challenge was trying to make food that was tasty enough for the Commander in Chief—that's another name for the President, I found out—and healthy enough for the First Lady.

"We're having a huge baking event in a couple of weeks," Mr. Quimby said. "Gingerbread houses." He showed me pictures from previous years. They were amazing.

Then he pulled out a tray of cookies and sat the platter in front of us. They were the best chocolate chip cookies ever!

"You have to give me the recipe for these cookies!" I blurted out.

Chef Quimby laughed. "Tell you what. You share your top cupcake recipes and I'll think about passing along my cookie recipe."

I took another big bite of cookie and licked my lips. "Deal!"

Next thing I knew, Mom, the First Lady, Chef Quimby, and I were posing for pictures together while eating Christmas cookies. *How cool is that?!*

By the time our visit was coming to an end, I needed a few minutes to myself to take it all in. I asked Mom if I could go to the restroom, and Miss Letitia directed me to follow her. We went around the corner, but the restroom she took me to was under construction.

"Take the elevator right here to the next level. You'll see it right there," said the maintenance dude.

I hesitated. I didn't really need to use the bathroom. And truth was, sometimes elevators creeped me out. I guess the maintenance dude figured it out, because he grinned and said, "You'll be fine, miss. Go on."

He was right, of course. Smooth ride, one floor up. The restroom was nicer than my bedroom. I instantly took out my phone and snapped several photos.

Drawing a deep breath, thinking about everything

that had happened throughout the day, I did the only thing I could do:

A happy dance!

Watching my reflection, I bounced around and around, grinning like a kid in a candy store. This had gone from the worst day ever to the absolute best!

With everything that happened at the Capitol, I was sure I'd be scarred for life. Now, after meeting the First Lady and talking to her, I felt like everything that happened might just turn out okay. And changing my mind about my future was okay, too. I made myself stand up straight, and stared into the mirror.

You are a leader. You are a young woman. You are an entrepreneur. You are president of the whole sixth grade!

I tossed cold water on my face, dried off, and drew in a deep breath, then slowly released it. I did my best imitation of the First Lady's relaxed and confident stride into the hallway and pressed the down button on the elevator. When the security dude looked at me, I gave him my most mature presidential nod.

The bell for the elevator dinged and I got on. I was so lost in thought, I didn't notice who was already on the elevator.

"Hey," said a voice.

"Hey," I answered. It was a boy about my age. Maybe a year older. A man stood next to him. The boy was glancing up from his tablet and the man looked like he was just chilling.

The elevator began to move, then, abruptly, it jerked. Someone shrieked like a little girl. (Hmm...it was probably me.)

We stopped moving.

When the lights flashed on and off, the elevator shook. Almost immediately, my knees shook, too. Already it felt like the space was getting smaller and smaller.

Is it getting hot in here?

I pressed my back against the wall and bit my lip. All the cookies I'd eaten bubbled in my throat. I sank to the floor, my knees pulled up to my chest.

Did I mention? I was confident about a lot of things...but I really—REALLY—hated tight spaces.

The man looked at me. "You okay?"

I just stared. Then a voice came through the speakers:

"So sorry about this, folks, but it appears there's been a hiccup in the power. Hold tight!"

The boy knelt down beside me. "It'll be okay," he said. I glanced at him. He looked familiar, but I couldn't tell from where. He had close-cropped hair and skin the color of pale caramel. Then, for the first time, I caught a whiff of chlorine.

The man started talking into his sleeve. A hidden microphone. All I heard was "mumble, mumble, mumble" then "Yes, sir, we're trapped inside. Yes, sir, Neptune is secure."

17

Neptune

It was the President's nephew. Code name Neptune. He looked a little older, more laid-back than in the photo Becks had saved on her phone. He slid down to the floor. We both sat with our backs to the wall, our knees bent. He looked at ease, though I was ready to barf.

He didn't sound like a big shot when he talked. I felt myself redden. It was so embarrassing, being in there with him. Not, like, romantic or anything. It was just that here I was, having the greatest day ever, then I had to go and step into a lethal deathtrap elevator and start shrieking like a preschooler. AND THEN I'm looking this boy in the face but remembering that stupid photo of him in those skimpy swim trunks.

He told me his real name was Frederick Douglass London. He said he was named after the famous African American abolitionist Frederick Douglass. "Most people either call me London or Neptune."

"Sorry," I mumbled.

He said, "For what?"

I gave him a "nice try" look. "You know," I said. He didn't seem to mind, though.

I think the Secret Service guy, on the other hand— I knew from Mr. G.'s class that that's who protects the president and his family—was afraid I might have a heart attack and explode dork guts all over the President's nephew.

I☆I☆I☆I

A little time passed, then Neptune asked for my phone number. I raised my eyebrow at him, but gave him the number. After that we started texting each other.

He was smart. Smart enough to know that if I was trying hard to concentrate on typing, I wouldn't flinch every time I heard a clink or moan of the motors and gears.

Neptune's fingers danced across the keypad.

```
NEPTUNE: Everybody's afraid of
    something.
ME: Not really.
NEPTUNE: Really.
ME: So, what are you afraid of.
NEPTUNE: Public speaking.
```

I looked at him. Laughed.

I said, "No way!"

"Yes way."

I pulled my clipboard out of my book bag. "I'm working on a speech. I'm not afraid of speech giving, but I'm sure no fan of speech writing."

He laughed. "I'd rather write a speech than give a speech any time. What's yours on?"

I let out a deep sigh. Lights flickered and the Secret Service dude mumbled into his shirt some more. Neptune was so chill, he could have been taking a nap. I knew he was talking to distract me from my terror. Every so often we could hear dings and pings from the workmen. To me it sounded like they were slapping the elevator around to keep us from falling to our deaths.

Inhale. Exhale.

NEPTUNE: Hard to give a speech when you don't know what it's about.

ME: I know the topic. Just hard to know where to start. In D.C. for a leadership conference. Class presidents expected to discuss power with purpose . . .

NEPTUNE: You're class president?

ME: President of the whole sixth grade.

NEPTUNE: That's legit.

ME: They let you use slang in the White House?

NEPTUNE: Just in the elevator. Or underwater.

We looked at each other and started laughing. The Secret Service dude rolled his eyes. He said, "Are you two really text talking when you could be talk talking?"

"Talk talking? That's a good one, Adam," Neptune said. He looked at me, and typed:

> NEPTUNE: Ignore him. What's your
>   purpose? As class president.
> ME: So far my biggest goal has been
>   raising enough money for trip
>   here.

I looked at Neptune and said, "What I stand for beyond that...what we hope to accomplish, that's what I'm not sure about. I wanted to do my speech on entrepreneurship. About the power of owning a business and making money and saving money, the importance of that."

His fingers stopped moving. He looked at me. "So why not do it?"

I shrugged. Something about it just didn't seem quite right.

We spent the next few minutes texting back and forth some more. I told him how my classmates made me feel heartless because I wanted to grow up to earn a lot of money. He said he wanted to earn a lot of money, too.

NEPTUNE: So you want to be a businesswoman?

I turned to look at him and said, "I am a businesswoman!"

He gave a half grin. "Is that right? What kind of business?"

ME: Cupcakes. Sell at a local bakery.
NEPTUNE: Want to be a pro chef?

His question led to another pause. I explained how I used to want that more than anything, but now I wasn't sure.

I did know one thing for sure, though. "I...want to make a difference."

He said, "You can do both, you know. Make money and make a difference."

"I like motivating people. The problem is, I also like the idea of having millions and millions of dollars in the bank."

"Why is that a problem? A lot of wealthy people do a lot of good. Look at Bill Gates or Paul G. Allen. They give away millions and millions of dollars."

"Well, one of the classes I really like is journalism. I love storytelling. But I don't know if I want to be a reporter, or an author—or both. Maybe even a filmmaker."

He paused to think for a minute. "Last year, Aunt Kaye held a luncheon on literacy here at the White House. The woman who wrote the Harry Potter books..."

"J. K. Rowling?"

"Yeah, her. She was here. She gives a lot of money to charity, too. There are a lot of ways to make a difference, Brianna Justice. You just have to pick one."

A voice came through the speakers again. "It'll only be a couple more minutes, folks."

Neptune and I sat in silence for a few seconds. Then I caught him looking at my clipboard.

"What?"

"Um, you know you could keep all your notes and dates and schedules in something like this," he said, waggling his tablet in my face.

I sighed. "Yeah, that's what everybody tells me."

"So, why don't you have one?"

"My aunt Tina says there's nothing like using good old-fashioned tools. She says there's nothing wrong with paper and pencil."

He rolled his eyes and laughed. When he laughed, he tipped his head back and closed his eyes. He was sitting so close, I could feel the muscles in his body contract and expand. I realized that he felt warm, and sitting next to him was . . . comfortable. Nice.

He said, "Ahhh! So you have one, too."

"One what?"

"An aunt who thinks she's always right!"

I frowned. "Hey, you can't talk about the First Lady like that. She's my new bestie." I flipped my phone's home screen to my photo gallery and showed him the pics of me and her with the chef and in front of the Christmas tree.

"Nice." He laughed. "But I wasn't talking about Aunt Kaye. My other aunt. Maddie. She's always into something. That's where I'm heading now. To the Capitol building, because of her. She drives my grandfather nuts."

"Yeah, well, my grandfather says Aunt Tina wouldn't have time for so many sayings if she got married."

We both laughed.

Then I looked over at him. "Is it hard? Living here, I mean. People all in your business all the time. Photos..."

Before I could even finish, I felt his muscles tense again. "Sorry. Really, sorry about that. None of my business. I shouldn't have asked..."

But he was already shaking his head. "You saw it, right?"

I looked away. "No," I lied. "Saw what?"

He laughed. "You wouldn't be this uncomfortable if you hadn't seen it." Then he leaned over and nudged me with his shoulder.

"Okay, so I did see it. I mean, yeah, it's your swimming uniform and all. But..."

"But what kid wants to look in the national newspapers or magazines and see a photo of his skinny legs sticking out of a Speedo?"

"Yeah. And your hair is so different, too. I didn't recognize you at first."

244

"That was the whole point. I thought if I got rid of 'that mop,' as Uncle calls it, I could go incognito. I haven't taken a lot of photos since it's been cut, but it's only a matter of time before word spreads."

"Does that suck? The word spreading, I mean."

He shrugged. "Being able to live here is a privilege. I'm not going to give up swimming just because a photo embarrassed me. I love to swim. I'm good at it, too."

I said, "I read that you grew up in California. Then when your uncle got elected, you moved here. Right?"

He nodded.

"Was it hard to start over? I mean, I know it's a privilege and all that. But...I bet you had friends. You had hopes and dreams long before you knew you'd be living in the White House. How did you handle moving and giving up your friends?"

He was silent for a moment and I figured I'd pushed too much. Sometimes I just didn't know when to shut up.

Finally, he let out a long sigh.

He said, "When Uncle Bill first sat me down and explained he was running for President, I thought it was great. I was so excited. For months, I traveled with him and my aunt, went and listened to his speeches. He was amazing.

"Then, when he won, I felt like I was drowning. I know it sounds crazy, but it was like the idea of us moving and our lives changing hadn't really occurred to me. All of a sudden, it hit me. I was leaving California. Leaving my old swim team. Leaving my best friends in the whole world."

He stopped talking. The pause was so long, I swear I could feel his pain through his skin. He drew in a breath and when he exhaled, his eyes seemed to be looking back in time. Probably to that day when he realized how much his life was going to change.

"Mike and Taz. They were my boys. Me and Taz had been swimming together since our mothers put us in Mommy and Me classes at the Y. My mom died when I was five. She had been an Olympic swimmer. Being in the water, after she died, it made me feel close to her. Swimming with Taz and, later, Mike, made me feel like somehow Mom was still there."

This time, he dropped his head. I touched his arm lightly.

"Neptune, it's okay. You don't have to explain," I said, noticing the sadness creeping into his expression.

"You know what, Brianna Justice? You're the first person I've ever told that to."

We both looked up at the Secret Service guy. He concentrated on his phone like he wasn't listening.

Neptune laughed. "Anyway, we've been in Washington almost two years now. I'm on a new swim team and I've made new friends. So, I guess, it's all good."

It should have lightened the mood, but all of a sudden I felt stupid tears starting to burn the corners of my stupid eyes.

In a whisper, I asked: "But do you wish you could just turn back time? Do you wish you didn't have to change? That things could stay the same?"

He thought about it for a minute. "You know what? At first, I did. I really did. Then one day last year, last summer, I was traveling with my aunt Kaye. As the First Lady, she does a lot for arts programs and art education. But she asked if I'd like to participate in an effort to teach more kids how to swim."

"I think I remember reading about that. At least, Grandpa read it to me. Just so you know, he loves your uncle!"

"Thank you. Anyway, we were going to different cities, talking to groups of kids. And in Fort Lauderdale, we went to this one park. I wasn't giving speeches, not to big groups, but I did talk to a few kids. This one little dude, I showed him what to do if he ever fell in a pool and didn't know how to get out. Well, several weeks later, they contacted Aunt Kaye and told her that the same boy got pushed into a pool maybe three weeks after we left. He managed to get to safety and he said it was because of what I showed him."

"Really?" Now I was smiling, too.

"Yeah. So, you know, I think about that. When I'm having one of those days when I wish things could just go back to the way they were, I remember that little boy. And I think, Uncle Bill won't be President forever. I'll go back to California eventually. Until then, maybe I can do something cool or make a difference for somebody else."

Neptune glued his face to the tablet again. After a few seconds, he pushed it in my direction and said, "Here. If you want, you should look up famous speeches in history. Might give you some ideas about how to deliver a great message."

We spent the next ten minutes reading lists of the best speeches ever. One of my favorites was Susan B. Anthony's speech in 1873 about the right for women to vote. John F. Kennedy and Dr. Martin Luther King Jr. were on there, too.

I felt a little overwhelmed. "But... all of these people were talking about big, huge, important things. I'm just a sixth grader from Detroit. I don't have anything big and important to say."

The elevator shook, and I shrieked. Again. Almost jumped in Neptune's lap. Then we were moving and before I knew it, we were back on the first floor and the doors were opening and a bunch of people were crowded around the entrance. Mom was right there and I spilled out of the elevator and into her arms. She started stroking my forehead, then announced to the whole wide world, "My baby has always been a little nervous of closed-in spaces."

"MOM!" I cried. But of course all the grown-ups thought it was funny and I didn't know whether to laugh or cry. To the right, I caught a glimpse of the First Lady. She was standing with Miss Letitia.

A big voice rose above the others and I turned.

"You all right, my boy? Thought I might have to send in a SEAL team to save you."

I looked at Neptune. He ducked as the man reached out to brush his hand across the top of his head.

It was the President. Of the United States. Of America!

I whispered to Mom, "Why would he send seals to save us? What does that mean?"

She squeezed me. "He means an elite branch of the United States Navy. It stands for Sea, Air, and Land teams. When the President needs to get someone out of a tight spot, that's who he calls."

"And who do we have here?" asked the President. He was coming toward us and I didn't know whether to step out of Mom's hug and shake his hand or run and hide. But I figured I'd had enough crazy for one day, so I reminded myself to be calm, cool, and sophisticated.

I stepped forward and held out my hand. "Hello, Mr. Brianna. My name is President."

He smiled. I groaned.

He said, "I think I get the idea. So, I hear you're interested in politics."

Now I glanced nervously at his wife. She smiled warmly.

"William, don't put the girl on the spot." She looked at me. "But, honey, any second now all these people in suits are going to sweep him away to his next meeting. If you want to ask your question, now's the time."

It was like a scene out of one of those movies. I swear to goodness, everything stopped.

Some opportunities only come once in a lifetime. Who knew when I'd get a chance to interview the President again.

I gulped. Pulling up my clipboard, I asked, "Would you mind if I quoted you? It's for my school paper. The First Lady already let me interview her."

"Fire away, young lady," he said.

"Well, it's a two-parter."

He said, "Darling, I've yet to meet a reporter worth her salt who didn't have a two-parter for me. Go on with your question."

I said, "What advice would you give on how to be a good leader? Um, wait. No. How to be an effective leader?"

He stared at me for a long time. It was getting a little nerve-racking standing there.

"You know, the secret to effective leadership is simply understanding what your strengths are and being smart enough to surround yourself with the right people.

Not only your friends, but people who care about your message and share your passion to take that message to others. Now, what's the second part of your question?"

I was writing as fast as I could. From behind me, I heard Neptune mumble, "You'd be done by now if you had a tablet." I turned and made a face.

"Okay, thank you for that, sir, Mr. President. Part two: If you want to take the message to the people, what are some strategies for giving a good speech?"

He gave a lopsided grin. "That's easy. Keep it short and simple and make them feel good about your message. I once heard Maya Angelou say that people may forget what you said or what you did, but they will never forget how you made them feel. Every good speaker must understand the truth of her words."

Then he was off. Mom hugged me as the President kissed his wife, waved to his nephew, and then allowed himself to be led away by a group of suit-clad men and women.

I felt someone walk up alongside me. Neptune.

"You do have something important to say," he said. "And people will listen. You just have to have the courage to say it."

Civics Journal
Ancient Rome and Middle School

The original Neptune was the god of the sea. He was beautiful and flashy.

According to one version of the myth of Minerva and Neptune, both gods favored a coastal village. But the villagers were afraid to choose between them. They feared whichever they chose, the other would be angered.

The gods decided to offer gifts to the townspeople. Whoever gave the best gift would be the winner.

Neptune gave the gift of a beautiful waterfall. However, when the people drank from it, they had to spit it out. It was salt water.

Minerva gave the gift of a gorgeous olive tree with the most amazing olives.

The townspeople loved it, but felt that a coastal village could not risk angering the god of the sea. So they didn't tell her it was the best gift.

But it turns out Neptune was pretty cool. He laughed and proclaimed Minerva's gift the best.

From that time forward, the olive tree remained a symbol of Minerva's gift.

I like the message behind that. Sometimes you can't be afraid of going after what you want.

And if you have power, use it in a way that empowers others.

18

Gladiators

Wednesday, December 10

Uncle's voice boomed through my cell phone. I was lying on my back in bed, arm thrown over my face, covering my eyes. Ebony was singing in the bathroom and Lauren was doing sit-ups between the beds. Red was doing ballet stretches.

"Morning, sugar," he said. "Missed you at dinner last night."

"I had such a long day yesterday. What's up, Uncle?" I fought back a yawn. Normally, at home, I'd already be up at this time, working at the bakery. My brain clicked on like a computer. I started mentally visualizing my "To Do" list.

He laughed. "Sugar, I thought maybe you'd like to come by later this morning. Do some baking."

That woke me up. "I have a new recipe I'd like to show you. Maybe I could teach you a few things."

He laughed, a loud barking sound. "Now you sound as crazy as your daddy. Must be where you get it from."

"Must be." I smiled.

"Anyway, I'm stuck with a kitchen full of ingredients I don't have room to store because my big shindig I was telling you about got canceled. It's a good time to try something new!"

I raised onto my elbows. "Oh, no! Uncle Al, I'm so sorry to hear that."

"I know, sugar. I know. Anyway, maybe sometime after breakfast, later in the morning, if you get a break in your schedule, come by and see your ol' uncle. Maybe I can learn a thing or two. Or maybe I'll knock you on your butt."

"When it comes to cupcakes, Uncle, you ain't ready for this!"

Who says bakers can't smack-talk!

I☆I☆I☆I

By the time I hung up, my three roommates were dressed and at the door. A sliver of daylight shone between the heavy drapes, but when they opened wider, I saw the ground covered in snow.

Now they stood at the hotel room door, holding their coats and hats, looking back at me.

"Want us to wait for you?" Lauren asked.

I shook my head. "I'll try to meet you down there."

As they were leaving, I called out to Red. "Hey, wait a minute. Can I ask you something?" The other two said they'd wait at the elevator.

Red was smiling, but her eyes didn't look right. She looked tense.

"What's up? Everything okay?" I asked.

"Oh, it's awesome," she said in her typical tone that said she meant the opposite.

"Why so awesome?"

She let out a sigh. "The usual. My demon ballet teacher sent me a text last night saying if I didn't get back soon another dancer may have stolen my lead."

"Evil witch!" I said.

"The evilest."

Although she was doing her usual cool act, I could see that the text message really bothered her. On an impulse, I gave her a big hug.

"I'm really glad you chose to come on this trip and get to know everybody better," I said. "It means a lot to me. But I sure hope you don't lose your spot because of this."

She shrugged. "Devil woman's tricks don't work on me. If that other dancer was so good, she would've won the spot two weeks ago. I'm good. But thanks, Justice. See you downstairs."

She left and I pushed myself out of bed, went into the bathroom to get ready.

Water shushed from the faucet. I spat out minty foam, then reapplied more toothpaste. Aunt Tina always said the best weapon was a great smile. A yawn escaped my mouth. I had stayed up late writing my speech after the other girls had gone to sleep. But it was worth it—I finally had something to feel good about.

The phone by the bed rang.

"Brianna!" said Mr. G.

My hair was tied up, wrapped in a scarf the way

the lady in the salon had showed me. Still had its blow-dried smoothness. (One thing you learn when you hang out with white chicks is that they can wash their hair every day. Some of them have to, because of oil buildup. Most black girls, though, would be bald if they washed their hair that much. Unless I got my hairdo wet, I'd be good for at least a week.)

The scarf was covering part of my ear. I was still trying to get it out of the way, but could hear Mr. and Mrs. G.'s voices, excitedly talking over each other.

"Hold on, please!" I said. It was too early for the G & G Show.

"Brianna! Have you heard?" said Mrs. G.

"You mean about the storm? Did something get canceled today?" We were supposed to have a full day of conference workshops this afternoon, after our Newseum trip.

"No," said Mrs. G., clearing her throat.

"Okay, yes. Our trip to the Newseum is on hold. Entire city has shut down because of the weather. But that's not why we're calling. Yesterday, at the Capitol, you guys sat in the Senate chamber and heard the senator's filibuster, remember? Well, she's still at it. She is attempting to set a world record for the longest filibuster on record." I could tell Mrs. G. was excited.

She took a breath, then pushed ahead. "We've already talked to several kids who'd like to head back to the Capitol with us. We wanted to see if you'd be willing to come, too. The senator is trying to draw attention to a pitiful lack of funding around the nation for technology programs in K-through-twelve programs."

"Um...okay," I said, because I didn't know what else to say.

Mrs. G. said hurriedly, "Brianna, this is big! Unless the states AND the federal government make technology in schools a real priority, kids like you and all the other Blueberries might face serious challenges when it comes to getting the very best opportunities in life."

When I told them I'd love to come along, Mr. G. said to meet them in the lobby.

After I got dressed and got to the lobby, Lauren came running over.

"Brianna! Did you hear? Someone at the Capitol building is trying to set a world record! We're going to watch."

She looked so excited, I couldn't help reaching

over to hug her. She hugged back and handed me two red apples and a Nutri-Grain bar. She shrugged. "You didn't eat this morning," she said. Red and Ebony came up next, also wearing coats and gloves.

"Look!" said Lauren, pointing at the gigantic television screens in the carpeted hotel lounge. It was the senator we'd seen yesterday. Letters crawled under her picture:

BREAKING NEWS: U.S. SENATOR ATTEMPTING TO BREAK RECORD SET IN 1957 FOR THE LONGEST RECORDED FILIBUSTER

Mrs. G. climbed onto a chair and clapped at us until everybody shut up. "Okay, students, this is a rare opportunity to watch how government works," she said. "We're going back to the Capitol building not only to see history being made, but also because we want you guys to really think about what's at stake. Now, be on your best behavior. Let's go, Blueberries!" Now I knew how amped up Paul Revere must've felt before riding through the streets of Boston. No, wait. More like Julius

Caesar rolling into Rome! Mrs. G. might as well have yelled, "Charge!"

When we stepped outside, we were greeted with the sparkling white glare from last night's storm. The air was cold and smelled like Christmas. Holiday decorations on the trees danced in the breeze.

As we walked to our bus, I noticed a few kids I didn't recognize from the conference making snow angels and laughing loudly.

Mr. G. saw me looking at them, shrugged, and explained that school was out all over the D.C. area. Lauren and I exchanged glances. It wasn't even that much snow. In Michigan, we'd have to go to school in that little bit of fluff. Just saying.

We all climbed aboard. I texted Mom. Most kids had to stick around to attend their workshops, but I was lucky not to have any until the afternoon. Mom was staying behind with several other chaperones to look after the bulk of our group while Mr. and Mrs. G. took ten of us over to the Capitol.

The ride had taken about seven minutes yesterday. Now it took close to twenty. Snow and ice crunched under the tires. We climbed out. Inside the visitors' center, we once again checked our coats and headed to Congressional Hall. But this time, entering the chamber was like entering another world.

Even though the room was large and deep with seating like a theater, it felt hot and cramped. Down at the podium, the same African American woman from yesterday, with her dark hair in a bun, was swaying to the beat of her own words.

"...*oh say can you see, from the dawn's early light...*"

I glanced at Mrs. G. "Why is she saying the words to the national anthem?"

"Because," Mrs. G. said, leaning forward like she was at the summer's biggest blockbuster and didn't want to miss a single word. "The rules of a filibuster are that a person can say anything as long as they keep talking."

"Why?" I asked. "What good does that do?"

Mr. G. explained. "The whole purpose is to disrupt the bill the majority wants passed. Remember what I told you yesterday, Brianna. A filibuster's primary function is to disrupt the proceedings. This is Congress's last session before breaking for the holidays. If they can't reach a vote by noon today, the bill will have to be shelved. The senator wants to stop the legislation and draw attention to her message. She wants funding for technology in K-through-twelve education to be a priority in state and federal budgets. All she needs is a little more time to get people on her side."

Ebony leaned over Mrs. G.'s shoulder. "Who are those people huddling close to her over on the other side?"

"Her warriors. Her gladiators," Mrs. G. said. She looked proud. "They are there to show they support her because they believe in what she's doing. You guys are witnessing history."

We watched for a while. I was mesmerized. The senator looked so strong and committed as she switched from the national anthem back to her topic that I wanted to root for her, too.

Glancing around the room, I eyed the other senators. Some would try to say things to throw her off her game, but Miss Filibuster was having None. Of. It.

A few senators looked so angry that their faces were red and their jaws trembled; a few dozed in their seats. You could tell some were totally behind the filibustering senator, and others wanted to ship her away to a desert island. The ones backing her up, her gladiators, were like her girls (and guys). Her posse.

Congress really was a lot like middle school. There were cliques. Rude people shouting over you. Others giving you the stank eye. And some who had your back no matter what.

The senator's voice rose, and I couldn't take my eyes off her.

"...if you can hear my voice, reach out, call your representative, call your senator, call everybody. The fact that we are even considering passing a nothing bill like the one before us, while our esteemed colleague Senator Howard Graham refuses to even listen to arguments that could amend it and add safeguards for education, is a travesty. So if you are listening, if you can hear the sound of my voice, call. Don't be idle when you can be active!"

The woman sagged a bit. I realized she'd been at this since we were here yesterday. Now it was almost nine thirty in the morning, and she looked dog-tired. Mrs. G. said if the senator wanted to break the record, which would help draw even more attention to her cause, she'd have to keep talking until noon.

There was an explosion of applause. Several female senators stood, clapping hard.

"What is her name again?" I asked.

"That's Madeline Wilson-Hayes," Mr. G. said. "She's the President's sister-in-law."

The President's sister-in-law.

Neptune's aunt Maddie.

"*... She's always into something,*" I suddenly remembered him saying.

"So this is who he was talking about!" I blurted out.

"What?" said Mrs. G.

"The President's nephew. He told me his aunt was raising a ruckus, but I didn't realize this was who he meant."

Mr. and Mrs. G., Lauren, Red, and Ebony stared at me. Then I realized what I said.

"Um, yesterday at the White House. Tell you about it later."

Gradually the senator pulled herself up, seeming to draw strength from her supporters. She looked ready to fight on.

And maybe I knew someone willing to help.

A picture popped into my mind. Along with an idea.

Was this the next chapter for *The Adventures of Cupcake Girl*?

Civics Journal
Ancient Rome and Middle School

The gladiators were these total warriors who often fought to the death in the Colosseum.

Some were slaves or prisoners, some were professionals. They had to fight with animals or one another for the amusement of the masses.

That is so totally like middle school.

Any time you stand out in middle school, you have to be ready for someone to throw a lion at you.

That's a hyperbole, but it doesn't seem too far from the truth.

19

The Roman Legion

"Mrs. G.? Can I go into the hall? I need to text some-one." I slid to the edge of my seat. A plan was churning in my brain.

She gave me a look. "Right now?"

"It's really important. I think I know how to help the senator!"

She looked at Mr. G. They both stared at me.

Mr. G. was, like, "You really met the President's nephew?"

"Uh, yeah. Long story. Can I tell you later?"

Everyone else had been listening, too, dying to know more. "You can tell ALL OF US later!"

I agreed and Mrs. G. gave me permission to step into the hallway. The guard outside the door went to the basket of cell phones and handed mine back.

> Uncle. U ready to bake? Want to help Sen. Wilson-Hayes with filibuster. U down with it? need to bake a LOT...?

A minute passed. Then two. I was getting jazzed about my idea. At the same time, I felt scared and excited and nervous all at the same time. My heart had turned into a marching band.

Three minutes passed.

Then...

> See her on TV now. Know her, good lady. Come! Sugar, let's bake.

I gave my phone back to the guard and slid back into the room. "Mr. G., Mrs. G!" I was so excited. "I have a plan."

"What kind of plan?" Mr. G asked.

"The senator said don't be idle, be active. So I need for *all* of us to get active. Come on, let's go!"

Once we were out the door and around the corner, I explained what I wanted to do. The senator had asked for people to join her in getting the message out about technology in the classroom. I liked that idea. And I didn't like thinking that by the time I was in eighth grade Mrs. G. or the journalism program might be gone.

I explained my idea:

We would go back to my uncle's restaurant and bake lots and lots of cupcakes. Then we'd trek them back over to the Capitol building and use them to attract attention from all the tourists and guests out on the mall. I figured if we baked for an hour, it'd be pretty crowded when we came back.

When we passed out the cupcakes, we'd ask people to get on Twitter or Facebook or whatever and show their support. If we could persuade other people to get their parents or schools to contact their congressperson and tell them how much they loved technology in the classroom, maybe it would give Senator Wilson-Hayes the votes she required. And in the meantime, maybe all the support would inspire her to keep going and beat that filibuster record!

But first, we needed to come up with our message. It was time to let the people know the sixth-grade Blueberries meant business.

When I finished explaining my plan, Mr. G.'s eyes got big. At first I thought he was going to tell me I was crazy. But before he could say a word, Mrs. G. ran down the row of us kids giving high fives like she was in the starting lineup for the Pistons.

"Brianna Justice! I've never been prouder," she said.

Then Lauren said, "That's my girl! Brianna. Let's go help the senator set a record!"

Everybody was cheering—well, whisper-cheering, because we didn't want to get into trouble. You know. For disrupting the Capitol and all.

Mr. G. grinned, but then his face got serious.

"Brianna, I love your idea. And your enthusiasm is great. I...we're behind you." He looked at Mrs. G.

before continuing. "However, if you do this, just remember that you may not finish in time to give your speech today at the General Assembly. That would disqualify you for your session with the magazine folks. So, are you sure?"

Oh, no! I'd forgotten all about that.

Everyone stared, waiting for my answer.

I could hear a television somewhere in the distance. It was the senator's voice. She was still hanging on.

I thought about one of the discussions we had in class about gladiators in ancient Rome. They were tough and fierce and didn't back down. I thought about the senator's speech. Listening to her made me feel like I had to do something.

It was time to be a gladiator!

"I'm sure," I said. "Let's go get our filibuster on!"

I☆I☆I☆I

Once we pushed through the double doors into the kitchen, Uncle Al was lining up bowls and spoons and ingredients on the table. He looked up and did a double take.

"What's all this?" he asked.

"My army!" I grinned.

I told him my plan and he started nodding.

"Sugar, I like the way you think. Everybody wash your hands and let's get a move on. We don't have long to work," he said.

I looked at the clock on the wall. It was almost ten. We'd need at least an hour to bake, cool, and frost.

"So, sugar, what's your favorite cupcake flavor?" Uncle asked.

I told him about the new recipe I'd been working on for a caramel-apple cupcake. When I told him what I needed, his large dark face split into a grin.

"Sugar! The group that canceled was from Michigan, like you. They had me ordering a boatload of apples. All we need are some peelers and some smashers," he said.

It took us a good ten minutes to figure out who would do what. Lauren and Mrs. G. left to go see if we had other classmates willing to help.

Ebony was all about heading up the social media. "Can't nobody tweet like me. Let me do it."

I looked at her and felt a warmth spread through

me. After that first meeting with her selling cupcakes at the football game, I kinda thought she was a total flake. Yet, here she was, right by my side, making it work.

With Mr. G.'s help, we came up with our message:

Don't be idle—be active! Support Senator Wilson-Hayes's filibuster. She's fighting for our future.

Mr. G. explained that the senator was trying to stop a bill that gave too much money to the businesses run by friends of other senators. He said Senator Wilson-Hayes wanted her fellow senators to give more money to schools for technology, and less to their buddies. We read our message back a few times. Mr. G. and Ebony said we needed a hashtag, too. The more times people used it, the more attention we would get for the senator.

We decided on #GetFilibustered.

Ebony started sending out messages and posting pics on Instagram, asking people to join us in front of the Capitol building at noon. She said we'd be handing out cupcakes "with the truth all up in 'em."

Mrs. G. and Lauren returned with Click, Romeo

James, and a few others. I couldn't help feeling a little disappointed that Sara and Becks didn't show up. But I pushed it out of my mind.

We got to work. The cupcakes required a caramel glaze, so I did that part; Uncle and Mr. G. used a special machine to remove the apples' cores. The batter called for less liquid since we were substituting apple into the filling, so we had to calculate that, too. Thanks to Uncle's super-large cupcake pans and multiple ovens, we were able to bake 150 cupcakes at once.

"Everybody, I need to get something from my room. Be right back!" I called out.

Uncle said, "Hurry back. I've got some miniature pie-pans just begging for my famous sweet potato pie recipe."

I called back, "Uncle, I'm in the cupcake business."

"Sugar, once I share this recipe with you, your business is going to change. Besides, I have a lot more stuff for little pies than I do for cupcakes. So get goin', then bring your butt back here."

Uncle was trying to get all up in my laurels. *Hmph!*

In the lobby of the hotel, several kids milled around. Not just from our school, either. Some other conference activities had been canceled because people driving in had been unable to come. I ran past and raced to the elevator. It didn't take long to get into my room, find my recipes, then zip back out.

While making sure the door locked behind me, I saw two people moving up the hallway toward me.

When they got closer, I saw who it was—Becks and Sara.

My first impulse was a big, goofy smile. I didn't think about being mad at them or hurt or anything. I was just flat-out glad to see them. Okay, so when I'd first left the White House I thought about texting them to tell them about meeting Neptune. Maybe I wanted to rub it in just a little. Then I thought about what Mr. President and the First Lady had said, how kind and generous they'd been. And most of all, what the First Nephew said about growing and moving on.

So I didn't text.

It had all been so much to think about in such a small amount of time. So I'd kept the whole White House thing to myself. And since turning into a gladiator and all, I hadn't had time to think about it.

And now here they were.

"Bree-Bree!" Sara called out first, running toward me. Becks hung back, looking down at her shoes.

"Hey!" I said. Didn't know what else to say. "What's up?"

When I got a good look at Becks, I could see that her eyes were red, like she'd been crying.

Sara looked from Becks to me and said, "Oh, Bree-Bree! You were right. Yesterday, at the mall, the Peas were like, 'Oooo! This is so cute' or whatever. Then they were all, 'Can you buy this for me?' So me and Becks, at first, were, like, 'No problem.' But Bree-Bree, soon as we spent our money on them, Prya used her phone and..."

Sara paused. Becks picked up the story. "Prya used her phone to record me trying to get into a pair of pants." Now it was Becks's turn to hesitate.

Sara went on, "And girl, they've already been showing it to people. Brianna, what are we going to do?"

At first, my heart did a skip-hop. *We*? As in us friends?

The idea made me feel happier than anything I could think of. But then I looked at them. Really looked at them. Sara was wearing yet another ridiculous outfit. Becks was looking angry and confused.

"Sara, I'm so sorry to hear that. The Peas are not

good people. But I've got to get back to Uncle's restaurant. Did you guys hear about the filibuster? We're making cupcakes to help this senator lady stick it to her opponents."

When Becks looked at me, her eyes were hard. "Oh? So you'd rather help some senator you don't even know than your friends?"

My cheeks felt hot. I could feel myself getting pulled right back into another argument. Sure, I was a gladiator, but maybe it was time I did a better job of choosing my battles.

"Like I said, I've gotta go. I wish you two would come help. We need you...." I said it as sweetly as I could. I tried not to have any judgment or I-told-you-so in my voice. Which was hard, because I really did have thoughts about the whole situation and wanted to yell, "I TOLD YOU SO!" real loud.

Becks huffed, "Let's go, Sara. I can't believe this!"

For a moment, I felt myself standing there, like I was caught on some sort of sticky web, hanging above the earth. They had been my friends for so long. We'd done so much together. I had hoped it could always be that way.

Right now, however, I knew who I wanted to be—and what I wanted to be. Coming to this conference was supposed to teach me about leadership. One thing I'd learned was that leading sometimes meant letting those around you do their own thing.

My stomach knotted a bit as I said, "I'm not sure what to tell you. I think you two need to talk to the Peas. Wish I could help, but I gotta run." Then before they could say another word, I was off, racing down the hall, jumping into a waiting elevator, and sprinting across the lobby.

I knew I had to do it that way. I didn't trust myself not to turn around and try to fix everything.

I☆I☆I☆I

The afternoon was a whirlwind.

At eleven, we trudged across an endless sea of whiteness carrying trays of baked goods. College kids from the senator's alma mater, Georgetown University, were on the plaza in front of the Capitol. They were competing to see who could make the most awesome snow sculpture, while cheering her on. Turned out, they were pretty impressed that a bunch of middle schoolers—sixth graders!—were trying so hard to make a difference.

Little by little, more people showed up. We kept tabs on the senator's speech. A lady from one of the TV stations came over and asked some questions. Then she interviewed me about what we were doing.

I told them the senator had asked for gladiators, so that's what we were. Since we were too young to vote, we were trying to encourage voters to show their support for Senator Wilson-Hayes and for schools. Ebony was a Twitter goddess. In no time she'd hooked up with teen groups and fangirls for various boy bands all across the country. Soon they were helping us, too.

After that, the whole scene turned into a carnival. People with signs, folks cheering and clapping.

C-R-A-Z-I-N-E-S-S!

It was nuts. And if that wasn't enough, one of the senator's aides came out and talked to Mr. G. She wanted us to know that Twitter was blowing up—in a good way. People from all over the country were listening.

"We have heard from several congressional offices that they are hearing from their constituents.

Apparently, a lot of teens are pushing their parents to take a stand. And the stand they want them to take is beside the senator. Thank you," she said.

When noon came around, I looked around and let out a huge breath.

We did it!

Every cupcake—gone!

Every pie—eaten!

Out on the steps of the Capitol building, we stood beside empty pastry trays.

At ten past noon we learned that the senator had killed the bill. At least for the time being. And she'd beaten the previous record for the longest filibuster in history.

And the record she beat? That was the icing on the cupcake. It was held by a senator named Strom Thurmond, who worked hard to prevent civil rights legislation. I might not know a ton of history, but you didn't grow up in Detroit without learning something about the civil rights movement. Can you say Rosa Parks? Hello!

Now we were practically being drowned by people cheering, and even more newscasters with cameras and microphones. Crazy, right?

A horde of the Georgetown students huddled up with us Blueberries as a TV camera pointed at us. Word of what we were doing had spread incredibly fast. Ebony and Mr. G. had mad skills when it came to social media.

Now they were asking us a bunch of questions. People were pushing. My heart was pounding. I'd never felt so tired—or so proud.

Then I heard a ripple of noise. Next thing I knew, someone was pushing through the crowd, approaching from my left side.

When I saw his face rushing toward me, I grinned. It was Neptune, with Adam the Secret Service agent close by his side.

"You did it!" he cried. Then he gave me a big hug. "You are awesome, Brianna Justice."

Yep, that was exactly what the president's nephew said. And he said it like "awesome" was really awesome.

Right after that, the scene went from mere chaos to absolute insanity.

And right in the middle of it was little ol' me. Didn't see that coming!

Civics Journal
Ancient Rome and Middle School

The Roman legion army wore very special uniforms. Along with the shield, armor, shirt, belt, and helmet, they also wore hobnailed sandals. The sandals were designed to make the maximum amount of noise and sometimes they even sparked against the ground.

Think about it.

Hundreds and hundreds of soldiers marching toward you so fiercely that their shoes even seemed like weapons.

Now that's awesome. My red Converse are cool, but they don't spark when I walk.

20

The Forum

We were rushed from one side of the House steps to the other. The news crews wanted me to make a statement. Mr. G. wanted me to make a statement, too. Not just to the media, but to the crowd.

I'd never had a problem with speaking in public, but now...now I was shaking in my Converse. And not just because of the ice and snow. When I looked down the steps, I was staring into a wave of faces. I was scared. All of these people were probably way smarter than me.

"Mr. G., I don't know what to say." My voice was hoarse and raspy.

He looked at his watch. "Brianna, you might not have time to make your speech at the conference. Here's your chance to make a different kind of speech. Are you going to take it?"

"I don't know what to say!" I repeated, steam hissing from my lips as my warm breath touched the cold air.

He took me by the shoulders and stared right at me. In science, we learned that if an animal in the wild does this, it's an act of aggression. For a brief moment, I feared Mr. G. might head-butt me.

He did not.

Instead, he said:

"Just tell the truth. Be honest. Let them see and hear your passion. Tell them how you feel."

I went back and stood before the crowd. One of the senator's aides who'd come out to join us had set up a podium.

Applause smattered, mingled with whistles, shouts of "woo-hoooooo," and expressions mostly of curiosity.

They were all waiting. For me.

I took a deep breath, then stepped to the microphone.

Just like in a movie, as soon as I got close to the

mic, screechy static sparked, making me wince. I was shaking. Then I looked out into the crowd and saw that Mom had made it over. She gave me a tiny wave and a nod. Then it was like she got swallowed by a sea of woolen bodies. People were shifting and moving. She appeared again, magically closer to the stage. Two wide-bodied dudes wearing long navy coats and dark shades stood on either side. I recognized them—her FBI buddies. Well, in case I was so bad that I caused a riot, the FBI might save me. Heart fluttering, I inhaled, then plunged into my speech:

"Miss...Senator Madeline Wilson-Hayes decided to change some folks' minds today. She made a call for gladiators. Gladiators willing to fight to make a difference. We learned about gladiators in Mr. Galafinkis's class. They are tough and strong and fierce. They get it done.

"Gladiators are not cowards. I used to think that people who were always trying to change themselves— like people at my school—were cowards. Scared to be themselves.

"Now I think maybe I was the coward. I was afraid of who I could become. That's not cool. Now I know I want to be a gladiator. Not just for the rest of the world, but for myself, too."

I paused to catch my breath. Looked around and saw people nodding their heads. Somebody shouted, "Go get 'em, little mama." My mom gave him her FBI face, and laughter ruffled the chill air. I took another breath and plowed ahead.

"That's why I knew I wanted to help the senator. While my uncle, teachers, and classmates helped bake the cupcakes and pies we passed out today—by the way, if you liked them, you should visit Uncle Al's restaurant, the Kitchen, or Wetzel's Bakery in Detroit. That's where I work. Anyway, as everyone was helping to bake or organize, I researched filibusters on the Internet.

"The dude who held the record for longest-ever filibuster was Senator Strom Thurmond from South Carolina. In 1957, Senator Thurmond didn't want things to change, either. So his filibuster was to block the Civil Rights Act. He did not believe African American people should have the same rights as other citizens.

"He was wrong. And he could not stop the change. The Civil Rights Act passed anyway.

"Like I said, today Senator Madeline Wilson-Hayes

called for gladiators. People strong and fierce enough to make the world listen. Her goal wasn't to just stop the bill from passing. She wanted people to take notice of what it failed to do. She wanted everyone to pay attention, to know that we need better technology education in schools.

"She is right. So, proud as I am about getting the word out, I still want to do more. The senator gave us a good start today. But what are we going to do tomorrow? We must keep making change!

"I came to D.C. excited to compete at our leadership conference. I was supposed to give a speech today that showed that the sixth graders at Blueberry Hills Middle School have a sense of purpose. I thought giving the best speech and winning a thousand dollars for our school would be cool. The most important thing ever!

"But then I met the President yesterday." I paused to take a breath. Murmurs began to swirl. I took another gulp of air and continued. "He's taller in person, by the way. Anyhow, he was nice enough to give me speech-giving tips. I thought, wow, I'm going to blow the competition away thanks to his suggestions.

"Well, I've missed the opportunity to compete against the other sixth-grade presidents at the conference. I will not win the thousand dollars for my school. And I will not get a chance to be featured in my favorite magazine in the whole wide world, *Executive, Jr.* Why? Because I chose to be here. And you know what? I'm good with that. Being able to be part of this. Setting a record, being with friends, learning and growing. Seeing how much I've changed already. And I met some great new people. So even though it didn't turn out how I planned, this is the BEST. TRIP. EVER!

"So, in conclusion, I will not fear change. I will seek it out and gladiate the heck out of it. I want to thank each and every person who reached out to help us today. I hope we all remember this day forever. If you want to change tomorrow, stand up for something today. My name is Brianna Justice and I am president of the whole sixth grade!

"I don't know what else to say, so I'm going to shut up now. And thank you!"

This time the applause was thunderous. It felt great. And delicious. And amazing.

Then there was shuffling. I heard some people gasp, then the next thing I knew, Neptune was at my side.

"Now this is legit!" he said as he pushed his way up the steps with Adam the Secret Service dude behind him.

About a billion flashbulbs flickered in our faces. Next thing I knew, a throng of Secret Service and FBI agents swarmed and led us inside the Capitol. It was terrifying and exhilarating.

Yet once we were locked away in a small office, I turned and looked at Neptune and we both just cracked up.

"That was intense!"

"Welcome to my world," he said with a grin.

We cracked up some more. Adam the Secret Service agent glanced at Mom and rolled his eyes. He said, "Your kid thinks she's funny. So does that one." He pointed his head toward Neptune.

Mom smirked. "Yes. While her height is taking its time, her snark is growing right on schedule!"

Adam answered a call, turning his back for, like, a second, then turned back and nodded to three other guys I hadn't even noticed.

People were all talking at the same time, and I felt a little light-headed from the heat of so many bodies.

Neptune tilted his head to one side and started moving toward the rear of the room. I followed.

"Soooo..." he said.

"Um, soooo..."

We laughed again, but this time, nervously. I started, "Thank you so much. For coming here, I mean. And for yesterday, too. You could've treated me like a total lump for freaking out on the elevator, but you—"

I didn't get to finish that thought.

Nope.

Because Frederick Douglass London, code name Neptune, was giving me my first kiss. On. The. Lips.

It tickled.

And my lips tingled.

The kiss was warm and brief. Not those long, gross kisses like the teenagers do on Nick at Night.

I looked up at him. I had the craziest urge to ask him if he liked my hair. What the what?

"Come on, scout," Adam said to Neptune. When he saw the look on my face—not to mention the look in Neptune's eyes—he hesitated.

Adam said gently, "Sorry, kiddo, but we've got to go. I'll give you two minutes, then we have to leave."

Neptune nodded.

When Adam left, Neptune turned back to me. "I . . . I hope you don't mind. I mean, what I did. I just, um, well. You're cool, Brianna Justice. It was nice meeting you."

It took several seconds before my voice came back. "It was nice meeting you, too."

We were just staring at each other like two dopes when Adam came back. He tapped Neptune on the shoulder and without a word, they both turned. And left.

I didn't even say good-bye. One second he was right beside me, the next he was gone.

My phone beeped and I read the message:

> NEPTUNE: Left you a package at hotel earlier. Check at desk. Stay in touch, Madame President :-)

When I looked up, Mom moved closer. "You okay, baby?"

I hugged her, feeling a rush of emotions. My face was buried in her jacket.

She gave me a squeeze. "I know, baby. Wait 'til I tell your father."

My head snapped up:

"Mom! He must never know!"

I☆I☆I☆I

By the time the six o'clock news came on, we were back at the hotel. Uncle helped Mom sneak me in through the rear loading dock because news crews were camped out front. When I made it up to our floor, several kids from my school—and other schools, too—stopped and applauded.

At first, it made me feel goofy. But after so much crazy stuff, it felt good to feel goofy. I did a big bow, then stood and waved.

That was when I noticed a guy with a sash across his chest. It said LEADERSHIP SPEAKER OF THE HOUSE! He must've won the award for best speech.

It was hard to believe that only a few days earlier the idea of winning that award was the most important thing in the world. I wanted to win because winning was important. At least, that was what I thought.

And I'd wanted to be featured in *Executive, Jr.*, because I thought it would help my cupcake business.

The idea of having to congratulate someone else because they'd won had been enough to keep me awake at night.

Now, here I was, facing the winner. And I hadn't even gotten to compete.

But I'd learned so much in the past few days.

I learned that finding your purpose isn't something you have to study or learn. Just something you need to feel. Purpose is just a way of knowing what is important to you and knowing what you can do about it.

Coming to D.C. was supposed to mean rebuilding my relationship with my friends. Instead, it meant figuring out that I had made new friends. And so had Sara and Becks. And as much as it hurt, that was okay.

I looked at the boy wearing the sash, stuck out my hand, and said, "Congratulations! Sorry I missed your speech."

He said, "Thank you! And congratulations on your speech, too!"

The rest of the night was spent having pizza parties

and dancing around with bedsheets tied over our clothes to look like togas.

Click came up to me, holding a little figure that looked like she was running for office. He clicked her plastic hair up and down on her head.

"Think it's time for a little moviemaking?" I asked.

Click! Click! Click!

Pretty soon, we had the whole party involved.

Click had brought along some LEGO pieces; he'd bought new ones since arriving in D.C.

I sat between Red and Romeo James on the floor at the foot of one of the beds. Lauren said, "Guess what's the world record for the largest full-scale model built with LEGOs? It's the X-Wing fighter and it contains five million three hundred and thirty-five thousand two hundred LEGO bricks!"

The whole room went silent for a second. We all looked at Lauren. Her face looked so happy. Her cheeks were rosy pink.

"Too bad they can't put your name in the record books with that senator lady," Romeo James said to her. He looked at me. "You, too, Brianna. Y'all rocked it. For real."

A knock at the door made us look up. It opened and Mom stepped in carrying a box.

She said, "This was at the front desk for you." She handed it to me and looked around. "Everybody doing okay?"

They were talking to her and she was talking to them, but I was just focused on what was inside the box.

I opened it, then read the card:

People say "stay in touch" all the time, but they don't really mean it. I do. Please stay in touch. It was good to meet you, Brianna Justice. Oh, and by the way, don't go getting any ideas just because I gave you this gift. I had like three of them, two I'd never opened. Consider it my donation to your business. Good luck.

It was from Neptune.

An iPad.

Well, naturally, everyone wanted me to explain

everything, going back to how I'd met the President's nephew while being trapped in an elevator. I may have added a few details here and there. You know? To make the story more entertaining. The one thing I didn't mention, though, was the kiss.

Although, I figured one day soon, I'd want to talk about it with Red and Lauren. My new girls.

I☆I☆I☆I

The very first thing I did with my new iPad was take photos of our LEGO creations. I had shown it to Mom, with the card, and after calling Miss Letitia at the White House, she said I could keep it!

Click had bought pieces to make his version of the National Mall. He used a lot of white bricks to make it look like snow and ice covered everything.

We were still in our bedsheet togas, lying on the floor.

"What're you gonna call your movie?" Ebony said.

To everyone's surprise, it wasn't me who answered. It was Click.

"To celebrate Brianna's love of crazy horror movies, as well as her love of politics, I dub thee *Sharks at the Mall!*" The National Mall, that is.

And with that, he made a plastic shark zoom into the air and fly right over a figurine of Abraham Lincoln.

We all cheered.

Everyone was still carrying on, laughing and having a good time, when someone else knocked.

"Can I talk to you for a minute, please, Brianna?" It was Sara. I got up, almost tripping over my toga, and followed her into the hall. She drew a deep breath.

She said, "I just wanted to say I'm really happy for you. You know, how everything worked out today. You were amazing."

I said, "Thank you."

It felt so awkward. How was it that someone I'd spent so much of my life with, all of a sudden felt like a stranger to me?

She said, "Look, I'm really, really, REALLY sorry about what happened at the Capitol. And in the hallway earlier. I just think... well, Becks..."

I shrugged, stopping her. "Look, don't worry about it. I'm sorry, too. You guys have a right to try to figure out whatever you need to figure out. I...I hope everything works out. For both of you."

She smiled.

I smiled back.

She said, "I think when Becks is with you, it just makes her feel like that same little dorky kid she was back in elementary."

My chest felt tight. Our times in elementary school were some of the best memories of my life.

I took a deep breath and said, "I understand." I didn't, but I wanted to.

We hugged, and Sara said, "We're still friends, though, right, Bree-Bree?"

"Always," I said. "But maybe you could just call me Brianna from now on?" I winked.

Then I watched her as she walked down the long narrow hallway, moving farther and farther away, until she simply vanished. Like she'd never been there at all.

Civics Journal
Ancient Rome and Middle School

Back in ancient Rome the best speakers were the ones who gained the most popularity.

It's, like, imagine if they had YouTube back then. The senators with the hypest channels or videos would have gotten the most play.

In other words, you had to have some serious game. Be able to talk about stuff and make it happen.

The Forum was where it all went down. It was a big open-air market where all sorts of people gathered, the rich mingling with the poor. Plebeians gathering to hear and be heard.

I had found my forum. And now I knew what being a good speaker was really all about.

Epilogue

Thursday, December 25

We had opened our Christmas presents and were sitting around eating chocolate chip cookies. Chef Quimby sent me his recipe and I totally rocked it. Dad was replaying part of the video he'd recorded of us opening our gifts, when the house phone rang.

Mom spoke into it for a few seconds, then said, "Brianna, it's for you!"

It was Senator Wilson-Hayes. "Well, Merry Christmas, Brianna Justice!"

It was the third time we'd spoken since her record-setting filibuster. She called right after we left D.C. to thank us all for our service. Then, in a news conference, she named Lauren Parker as being among the talented young people to help her set a new record. (I'd asked her to use Lauren's name to represent our group. Lauren had grinned for a week!)

"I know we talked briefly about it last time, but I just wanted to tell you once again that we are looking forward to having you help us when we come to Michigan next month," she said.

Since her filibuster, she'd started working with a group that held camps and workshops specifically targeting girls. The purpose was to expose more girls to science and technology. Lauren and I were going to help with the upcoming workshop, "Tech City Girls," being held at Wayne State University downtown.

"Well, I'll see you next month. In the meantime, there's someone else here who wants to say hello."

"Hey," Neptune said. I could hear his smile through the phone.

I grinned. "Hey."

We'd texted a lot since D.C. He had been practicing a ton for the swim team. I told him about *Executive, Jr.* magazine featuring me in their online edition.

"Has it been easier to stay organized, now that you've come into the twenty-first century and ditched the clipboard?" he asked.

I said, "Don't go dissing my clipboard. But I've gotta admit, going digital isn't so bad."

"Change can be good," he said.

"Even when it feels scary," I answered.

We both paused, letting the silence fill in around us. Not uncomfortable, just, you know? Chill. Then he said, "Hey, the lemon cupcakes were amazing. Quimby served your recipe at the holiday reception here."

"He used my recipe? At the White House?"

"Duh!"

We both laughed. Mom came over, tapping on her watch. I told Neptune I needed to bounce.

"My friend Red that I told you about? She's dancing in the *Nutcracker* today. We're about to head over."

Again, I could just feel his smile.

"Now that's legit."

It was legit, indeed!

I hung up and scooped little Angel into my arms. She purred and I did my best ballet twirl across the floor. Only a week 'til New Year's Day. After everything that had happened over the past few months, for once I was more focused on what was ahead rather than what used to be. It felt good.

Angel cat licked at the crumbs on my pj's. She was looking forward to the future, too. As I cuddled her into me and ran up the stairs to get ready, my mind was busy.

What was next?

More baking?

More public speaking?

Maybe more stories in the school paper.

I pushed open my bedroom door. The cat leaped onto my bed, and my old clipboard tumbled to the floor. I picked it up and decided my future may not need more of anything, just less worrying about what was next.

Time to get dressed and see what would happen next.

Hmm... maybe I'd jot some things on the calendar on my new iPad. You know, just in case.

Brianna Justice
The Twelve Laws of Middle School

No. 1—Everybody needs to be included. Nobody likes to feel left out.

No. 2—No one cares how cool you were last year or whatever. Focus on what you're going to do next instead of trying to build a rep on who you used to be.

No. 3—"If you don't stand for something, you'll fall for anything." I got that quote from a local radio DJ who said he heard civil rights legend Malcolm X use it. I think where middle school is concerned, it is definitely true. In the spirit of Spartacus, don't be afraid to stand up for yourself or what you believe in. Even when doing so isn't easy. And don't be afraid to stand behind your beliefs, even if it means standing alone.

No. 4—Instead of feeling sorry for yourself and sitting around doing nothing, go out and do something for someone else.

No. 5—Think before you act. Being too impulsive can be costly, especially when you have something to lose.

No. 6—When you plan something with your friends, make sure everybody is on the same page. Don't assume they want the same thing you want.

No. 7—Always represent. When you're on a school trip, make sure people see you at your best. *Senatus Populusque Romanus*—SPQR—was the ancient Romans' way of working their brand, sending a positive message. So work your brand, and represent your school colors with class.

No. 8—Sometimes grown-ups really do have some good advice. Don't be afraid to ask people you respect to offer tips or guidelines about your situation. You might learn something, and being asked for help makes grown-ups feel all tingly inside.

No. 9—Absolutely remember to ask other kids for help. Don't ask people to take risks that you wouldn't take, but tell them that if you take the risk together, you can support one another.

No. 10—There is strength in numbers. If you have a cause worth fighting for, gather your troops and put your plan into action.

No. 11—Coming up with the perfect made-for-TV thing to say might sound cool, but when it matters, speak from your heart. People will appreciate your honesty.

No. 12—Let yourself believe in magic, at least a little. Really cool things can happen when you believe in yourself. Don't be afraid to dream, to hope, to believe.

Dear Chef Quimby,

A deal is a deal. Here are three of my favorite recipes. I hope you like them. I think the lemon is my favorite. Share it with Neptune, please. I mean, if you want to. It was great meeting you. Hope to see you again soon.

Brianna Justice

P.S. You don't have to follow all my instructions. I did that for beginners.

☕ The Perfect ☕
Caramel Apple Cupcakes

Cupcakes
Makes 18–24

4 medium peeled apples
2 eggs (room temperature)
½ cup unsalted butter (room temperature)
1 cup granulated sugar
¾ cup light brown sugar
1½ teaspoons vanilla extract
2 cups all-purpose flour
½ teaspoon salt
2½ teaspoons baking powder
½ cup milk
½ cup to 1 cup chopped pecans

Caramel Glaze*

½ cup honey
½ cup or 1 stick Land O'Lakes butter
    (best butter EVER for baking)
¾ cup light brown sugar
1 can condensed milk

(continued)

First, prepare your cupcake baking tins for 12 cupcakes. Spray with cooking spray. Be sure to spray the sides and the top or spray the top of the pan and slide cupcake liners into pan.

Preheat oven to 350 degrees. Grate apples into a bowl. Combine eggs and butter; beat with grated apples for 30 seconds to 1 minute. Add sugars and mix for another 30 seconds. Add vanilla extract.

In separate bowl, combine flour, salt, and baking powder.

Now it's time to combine the wet and dry ingredients. Gently add the dry ingredients to the wet mixture using a large mixing spoon. In between scoops of dry mixture, add milk. Once mixture is completely blended, inhale that awesome aroma. Love that! Okay, now it's time to scoop the batter into the cupcake tins.

Once each tin is full, top with pecans and bake for 18 to 21 minutes. Halfway through, check to make sure cupcakes are baking evenly. Bake until golden and toothpick can be inserted and removed dry.

*If you can, prepare your caramel glaze before you bake your cupcakes, so you're not too rushed and it has time to cool. (You can store it in a glass jar—just make sure to spray the inside with cooking spray first.).

Now this is so important: You must get a grown-up to help with this next step. The glaze will get sticky and hot. Trust me! You do NOT want to get this on your skin while it's hot.

In a saucepan, combine honey, butter, and sugar. Over a low flame, have a grown-up stir the ingredients until mixture comes to a rolling boil. What is a "rolling boil"? That's just another way of saying, like, when those little bubbles start to appear because the mixture is getting hot, but hasn't started to completely boil. Anyway, when it begins its rolling boil, add the milk and continue to stir. Keep stirring until the honey and buttery sugar mixture are an even, milky shade of brown.

When your cupcakes are ready, crisscross them with the caramel glaze. If you want an extra-yummy experience, top with either a cream cheese or chocolate frosting.

Oh, man!

🧁 *The Ultimate* 🧁 *Chocolate Frosting!*

1 package (8 ounces) Philadelphia cream cheese
    (you can use other brands, but I like this one!)
1 stick Land O'Lakes butter (again, my fave!)
½ cup mini Nestle's chocolate morsels
2 cups confectioners' sugar
1 cup Hershey's unsweetened cocoa
¼ teaspoon vanilla extract
¼ cup milk

Okay, here's the deal. How to make the best frosting ever:

Start by letting your cream cheese and butter soften. DO NOT MELT. Just leave them on the counter in your kitchen for about an hour before use.

Place the cream cheese in a bowl and use a mixer to cream the cream cheese. I know that sounds funny, cream the cream cheese. But you've gotta do it. Beat it with the mixer for about 30 seconds.

Now add the butter. Blend the two for at least a minute. Set aside.

In a microwave-safe bowl, add the chocolate morsels. Here's something else that sounds funny.

You have to sweat the morsels. Weird, right? All that means is you need to add a few drops of water and place in the microwave for 30 seconds to a minute.

Add the molten chocolate to the creamed mixture. Blend for 15 to 30 seconds.

Now it gets fun. Start adding confectioners' sugar and cocoa. Add a little of each at a time. Mixture will start to become thick.

Add the vanilla extract and the milk. Blend until all ingredients are smooth.

It's time for tasting.

Mmm-mmm good!

☕ *Lemon with* ☕
Love!

Okay, so lemon may not come to mind when you think of the holidays, but my new friend Toya told me she loooooooves lemon. So of course, you know me, I had to hook the girl up. After a couple of tries, I came up with the perfect simple recipe for lemony goodness.

Cupcakes

zest from 3 medium-size lemons, divided
1 box Duncan Hines lemon cake mix (or another
    lemon cake mix is fine)
½ cup lemon juice, divided
3 eggs
¾ cup water
¾ cup vegetable oil

Frosting

½ cup butter (room temperature)
1 package (8 ounces) Philadelphia cream cheese
    (room temperature)
½ teaspoon lemon extract
½ teaspoon vanilla extract
3 cups confectioners' sugar
⅛ cup milk

First, start with the cake mix. Follow the instructions on the back of the box, using the eggs, water, and oil. However, ONLY USE 3/4 cup water, not a whole cup, as most packages call for. You will be adding lemon juice, so you have to reduce the amount of water so the mixture won't get too soupy. Add the vanilla extract, 1/4 cup lemon juice, and 1/4 cup lemon zest. Lemon zest is what they call it when you take, like, a cheese grater and rub it along the skin of a lemon. Take the pulpy lemon that comes off the skin and drop into the batter. I know, it sounds weird, but trust me, it works.

Now your kitchen oughta smell all lemony and bright. Scoop batter into cupcake tins. (You should have already placed liner cups in the pan or sprayed with cooking oil to avoid sticking.) Bake according to package.

Meanwhile...

This frosting is so good.

Place the cream cheese in a bowl. Use an electric mixture to cream the cheese. Get it nice and mushy. Now add the butter. Cream the two together for two minutes.

Add 1/4 cup lemon zest, 1/4 cup lemon juice, and the lemon extract.

Now add the confectioners' sugar, one cup at a time, blending between cups. Alternate drops of milk with the sugar to keep sugar from clumping. Mix until smooth. Chill until ready to frost cupcakes.

Yum!

Acknowledgments

I would like to dedicate this novel to my sisters, Jennifer and Janice, whose unending support has upheld me throughout the years. To my daughters, Lauren and Kenya, who make me laugh when I don't want to, and hold my hand when I need them most.

Also, I would like to thank Kathleen Vokes and the late George Nicholson from Sterling Lord Literistic. For your energy and patience, thank you so much.

And lastly, to my newest editor at Little, Brown, Allison Moore: I cannot express my gratitude for how you've guided me. I think we work well together and can't wait for our next project. Sincerely, Allison, it's been great working with you.

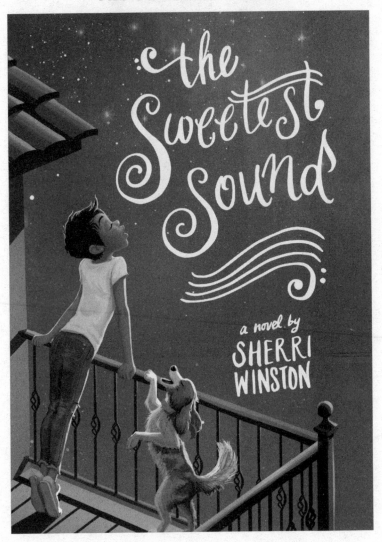

Turn the page for a sneak peek!

Prelude

Birthdays are a problem for me. It's been that way for almost four years. My seventh birthday was the last time life felt normal. My party was amazing. We ate dinner at a Mexican restaurant, just family and a few friends—the way I like it. One of my friends, Faith, is from the Dominican Republic, so even though people assume she's African American, she speaks Spanish quite well, thank you very much! She taught us some words. The band played "Happy Birthday to You!" the Spanish way, and we sang *"Feliz cumpleaños a ti."* The music felt like sunshine on my skin, and Faith, Zara, and I did silly dances. My mother even sang with the band.

It was the best night. Just the absolute best!

The next morning I found a note on the coffeepot. It read:

> *I love you all so much. But I have to pursue my passion. I can't grow in Harmony, can't be a star here. Jeremiah, you are a great man, wonderful husband, and terrific father. Cadence and Junior are lucky to have you. You deserve to be loved more than I can offer. Please don't hate me. Cadence, my sweet little Mouse, so quiet and shy. Always remember, you are the high note of my life. I will always love you.*
>
> *Chantel Marie Jolly*

And then, she was gone.

Birthdays have been tricky ever since.

My name is Cadence Mariah Jolly.

I live in western Pennsylvania in a small town called Harmony.

I'm up in the middle of the night because I simply cannot sleep. Last year I stood outside my bedroom on this very balcony, staring past the dark mountaintops, pleading for a miracle. If God answered my prayers it would be a sign. No more sad, weird birthdays.

That's what I thought. Truly.

Funny thing, though. God answered my prayers. I got exactly what I wanted.

Now, four weeks away from my next birthday, that blessing feels more like a curse.

I read a book over the summer called *Holes*. It was about this kid, Stanley Yelnats, who got sent away to an awful juvie place in the desert for something he didn't even do. Talk about a curse! It was a great book, and I've reread it a few times. I plan to be a No. 1 Bestselling Author of Amazing Stories one day, so I like to study the works of other authors.

I love reading, because authors have an amazing gift—they see problems and they find solutions. Have you ever wondered how an author would fix your life in a book? If the author of *Holes*, Louis Sachar, wrote a book about me, would he write about the fact that I'm really quiet? That at times I like being alone? Would he write about how I get this shaky, dry-mouthed feeling that makes my heart race whenever I'm around a lot of people? And if he did write a story about a girl like me, one who loves to read and plans to write great stories, a girl who is quiet yet tired of getting talked over and overlooked, tired of being pitied, how would Mr. Sachar fix her? (Me?)

Trust me. I've got lots that need fixing.

All I asked God for was one thing: for Daddy to find a way to get me a Takahashi 3000x keyboard and microphone. (It's the kind used by all the best Internet sensations! At least, that's what Faith says.)

In my prayers, I promised I'd share my secret talent with the world, if only God made my dream come true. My aunt and lots of people at church were always warning us kids about our prayers. *God ain't no Santa Claus,* they liked to say. *When you talk to the Lord, be mindful of what you're asking for. A prayer is a powerful thing.*

Honest, I believe in God, but truthfully, I wasn't quite convinced He'd even care about my keyboard or my secret.

Until it happened. God granted my wish. It was like some kind of miracle.

Somehow Daddy got his hands on a busted-up Takahashi 3000x and fixed it without me finding out. Next thing you know, I get the keyboard for my birthday. A real dream come true.

Now it's time to keep my promise. But I don't think I can.

What happens if you make a promise to God, then try to take it back?

1

Underneath the Stars...

Some words feel so grown-up when you say them. Like *scintillating*. I whispered the word like it was part of a magic spell. One of many astronomy terms I learned from my mother. It means twinkling like stars. When she taught it to me, she would say it, then tell me to repeat it, and touch my lips as I did. Said to let it tumble from my mouth.

My mother loved staring into the night sky. She loved pointing out groups of stars called constellations. She told me *I* loved it, too. Which was funny, because I could have sworn that staring into the sky at distant planets and glowing dust used to scare me. It made me feel so small, like I was vanishing. All I knew about the sky and the stars was what my big brother, Junior, had told me. Which was that slimy aliens and space monsters lived out there—he knew it because someone named Captain Kirk told him so. Like I knew the difference between Captain Kirk and Cap'n Crunch.

I told her once, my mother, that looking into the deep vastness of the sky made me afraid. She surprised me, saying it used to do the same to her. She said she'd wondered as a kid about the universe with all of its mysteries, but she figured its mysteriousness was part of its beauty.

She was so convinced that I loved it as much as she did that she ordered a telescope as a gift for my fifth birthday.

Don't get me wrong. I did get quite a few things that I loved, too. Such as a tiny iPod and multiple pairs of candy-colored earbuds. I love music. My favorite singer was (and still is) Mariah Carey. She is like my fairy godmother. If fairy godmothers were real, which they aren't. Except…maybe. I haven't quite figured that out. Anyway, I had listened to my Mariah playlist for so long, it was as if her songs were made to explain all the chapters of my life.

Later on, of course, my mother was gone, but the night sky no longer freaked me out. I gazed into the tiny lens of the telescope because seeing the stars up close made me feel closer to her. I knew that Captain Kirk was a make-believe character in *Star Trek*, and aliens and space monsters were make-believe, too. Probably.

I also knew that most of the time, especially lately, I was the one who felt like an alien. Staring into the heavens, I imagined stories about the planets and the moon. Outer space didn't make me feel invisible anymore; people did.

Darkness wrapped around me. I pressed my eyes shut and remembered the touch of my mother's fingertips on my skin.

When I opened my eyes, her image appeared in the sparkling mass of constellations. The shape of her face was Cassiopeia; her eyes, Polaris; the curve of her neck, the handle on the Big Dipper. Just the way I remembered her, before she left us. Beautiful and distant. *Scintillating*.

I used to get lost in the shadow of her shine. She was so beautiful and talented that it was like she cast this bright glow, you know? And the light from her amazingness reached way up into the heavens. I could never, ever come close.

When she left, our world slipped into darkness. Would it be that way forever?

Our house is three stories high. The top floor is like my apartment—I have it all to myself since my mother left and Daddy said he couldn't face being up here alone. He and Junior carted all my things up from the first floor because Junior said he didn't want to be up here, either.

Now it's just me and the last wonderful gift my mother ever gave me: my floppy-eared spaniel terrier, Lyra. She'd say hi, except it's late. Really late. And Lyra loves her beauty sleep.

Holding Lyra close, I leaned back on the chair and took in the night sky. My imagination conjured a familiar story. One that absolutely, positively made me sway. The way you might if you stood up too fast and got light-headed.

The story came out of my soul, and now it rests in a journal. All good writers keep journals. When I grow up, I will write wonderful stories about girls who are brave and wise and fearless. Girls unafraid to stand out. Girls nothing like me.

So, in the story I made up, my mother is no longer absent. She's returned. She is in awe of my writing talent. She loves me so much and wishes she had not left me back when I was a little kid.

We are being interviewed on TV. The host has tears in her eyes talking about my amazing new book. She says with a name like Cadence Mariah, it's no wonder my words flow like a song, no wonder I grew up playing the piano and singing in my school and church choirs. The TV host understands. *Cadence* means "rhythm." Middle name, Mariah, as in the famous singer, Mariah Carey. (See why I feel like she's my fairy godmother?)

Now, in my story, which flashes across the purplish mountainside like in a movie on a theater screen, I see the whole scene so clearly. I'm laughing with the interviewer, a quiet little laugh, and explaining how I used to be so shy that I hid in the back rows of the choirs.

My mother, I reveal to the talk show lady, is known throughout our hometown for sounding like the famous singer Whitney Houston. When I was born, Daddy says, she couldn't bear to share the perfection of Miss Houston with me. Instead, she made my middle name the same as her second-favorite singer, Miss Mariah Carey. But to me, Miss Mariah would always be No. 1!

The TV show lady, tears glittering in her eyes, begs the two of us to sing a song together.

My mother says, *No, she couldn't.* She says, *My baby won't sing because she is so shy.*

And then the TV show lady looks at me. Eyes pleading.

I walk over to my mother. I am very confident and sophisticated. The youngest bestselling author in the whole, entire world. She does not know how much I've changed since she left us. I am different now. Not the same Mouse.

I say, *Okay, Mother. I will sing with you.* In a totally low-voiced, dramatic sort of way.

And then we stand in the middle of the stage. My mother slips her hand into mine. Then the music begins.

The orchestra knows exactly what song to play. The only song that makes sense:

"When You Believe."

It is the only duet between the great Miss Houston and the amazing Miss Mariah.

When we begin to sing, my mother stares in disbelief. She cannot believe how beautiful my voice is. She always wanted me to be a singer. Like her. But I don't think she believed it would happen. I was always too shy. Was that why she left us?

She did try to be happy as a wife and mother, working part-time at the Superstar Gas n' Grocery Mart while taking classes at the community college.

But that kind of life was making her die inside, Daddy said. He said somebody like my mother was born for bigger things. He said we did not wish her ill, but would, in fact, pray for her success and joy and happiness. Like my mother, Daddy seemed to think he knew what I was feeling without even asking. And even though my mother sent me a phone as a gift, she rarely called or left a number where I could reach her. Still, I told myself that was okay. I would hold no grudges; I told myself I forgave her. In my heart, I hoped it was true.

So, in my story, my incredible, amazing, can't-put-down, make-believe story, there we are. Reunited.

And singing.

It is the best feeling in the whole wide world.

Sherri Winston is the author of *President of the Whole Fifth Grade*, a Sunshine State Young Readers Award selection, *President of the Whole Sixth Grade*, a Kids' Indie Next pick, *The Kayla Chronicles*, and *The Sweetest Sound*. She lives with her family in Florida. Sherri invites you to visit her online at voteforcupcakes.com.